"No m

Laurel was wriggling out of her dress even as she spoke.

"Hold on," Dane protested, a gleam in his eye. "This isn't a race!"

"But I saved the essentials for you...." She posed alluringly in her bra and panties. "Besides, haven't you heard? It's better the second time around."

"I was looking forward to enjoying the first." And with studied nonchalance he undid his belt buckle, sliding his pants downward.

Laurel breathed deeply, surrendering to the tenderness and love she felt for this man, as well as the desire. Pressing herself against him, she whispered "You're a tease" in his ear.

"And what are you, darling?" Dane's lips hovered over hers.

"I'm a natural woman ... with natural appetites."

The three years **Cassie Miles** spent in the Rockies, living in an isolated cabin, gave her the inspiration for this Temptation. Like her heroine she went all natural— baking her own bread, chopping her own firewood, coping when her outhouse exploded. Well, almost all natural. She never did quit smoking. Cassie now lives in Denver with her husband and two young daughters.

Books by Cassie Miles

HARLEQUIN TEMPTATION
26–TONGUE-TIED
61–ACTS OF MAGIC

These books may be available at your local bookseller.

Don't miss any of our special offers. Write to us at the following address for information on our newest releases.

Harlequin Reader Service
901 Fuhrmann Blvd., P.O. Box 1397, Buffalo, NY   14240
Canadian address: P.O. Box 2800, Postal Station A,
5170 Yonge St., Willowdale, Ont.   M2N 6J3

It's Only Natural

CASSIE MILES

Harlequin Books

TORONTO • NEW YORK • LONDON
AMSTERDAM • PARIS • SYDNEY • HAMBURG
STOCKHOLM • ATHENS • TOKYO • MILAN

Published April 1986

ISBN 0-373-25204-8

Printed in Canada

1

A MECHANICAL WHINE vibrated through the mountain meadow, startling bluebirds and sending chipmunks scurrying to their nests. Laurel Janeway knelt at the perimeter of the field, harvesting the wild mushrooms that grew beneath the conifers. She cocked her head at the sound. A chain saw? No, it was coming from overhead.

She rose, dusted her gardening gloves against her blue jeans and looked up, searching the overcast August skies for the source of this unnatural intrusion.

The engine coughed as she spied the strange little aircraft and recognized the hornet-shaped silhouette. It was one of those one-person recreational planes that looked as if the parts and pieces had come out of a Cheerios box. An ultralight.

She'd seen one on the ground at a private airfield west of Denver and had marveled at the aerodynamics that allowed a hobbyist to slap together a couple of pieces of balsa wood and attempt to duplicate the feats of Kitty Hawk.

Her pale-blue eyes fixed on the darting ultralight, and she clicked her tongue against her teeth in an old-fashioned tsk-tsk. Why would any sane person trust his physical well-being to something with the propellor stuck on the back instead of the front? That scrawny engine looked as if it belonged in a lawn mower, not an airplane.

Yet she had to admit this odd flying machine had its own sort of barnstorming dignity. With spunk and grace, it spiraled aloft. Vagrant rays of sunlight pierced the darkening sky to gleam on cherry-red wings. The plane fluttered through a lowering cloud, dived and soared, riding the unpredictable thermal air currents.

Free as a butterfly, she thought, and equally vulnerable to swats from turbulent mountain winds.

Though she hadn't subscribed to a daily newspaper since she'd moved to the mountains more than seven months ago, Laurel remembered reading about ultralight accidents. The stories were seldom longer than a few paragraphs and generally reported a fatality.

The droning aircraft circled the meadow, almost as if preparing to come in for a landing. That couldn't be, Laurel thought with alarm. Surely there was some mistake. Nobody would attempt to touch down on this rugged terrain, not even someone crazy enough to pilot an ultralight.

She dashed through the rye grass and wild flowers, her long blond braid flopping against her back. With hands cupped around her lips to shout a warning, she halted. What would she say? "Don't land here—this field is full of rocks and potholes"?

The pilot had to be aware of that. Anybody who'd walked ten yards in the Rocky Mountains knew the land wasn't a paved runway. Besides, even if she hollered until her face turned blue, he wouldn't be able to hear her voice above the sound of the engine.

Helplessly she stared up. This must be an emergency. She backed away, leaned against the trunk of a tall spruce and waited with slender arms folded over her soft flannel shirt. Her fingers balled into fists. What if the plane crashed? What if it burst into flames?

Though her log cabin was just over the second hill to the east, she was ill-equipped for disasters. No telephone. No nearby neighbors. Her only transportation was an ancient Jeep. She could try to contact someone on the CB, but it was only good for short-range communication. What if there was a serious injury? The nearest hospital was thirty-four miles away.

The ultralight plane cruised low, then climbed toward the spires of Ponderosa pine at the southern edge of the meadow. Laurel held her breath as she watched the wingtips barely clear the treetops.

The craft pirouetted in midair and swooped down for its final approach, riding on a draft of chill northern wind. The smooth descent ended in a fearfully bouncy landing as three wheels jolted over rocks and high brush. The light plane jumped almost a foot into the air before the right front wheel smashed against a tree stump with a loud crack. The bright red wings tipped precariously as the ultralight skewed in a full circle. The motor coughed and stopped. The propellor stilled.

Laurel raced across the field. Was everything all right? Was the pilot okay? Was the thing going to explode?

A gasoline smell tainted the clean, mountain air, and the aircraft sat as motionlessly as an injured sparrow. Its graceful flight had ended, perhaps forever. Through translucent windows, she saw the pilot slumped forward in the small cockpit.

A warning sense slowed her sprint, and she had a premonition of heartache so agonizingly deep that she halted. Reflexively her eyes narrowed in a wince, and her fingers in the gardening gloves twined together in a knot.

The pilot stirred. He lifted his head, looked in her direction and waved. Warm relief flooded through her. At least he was conscious.

As he unfastened his safety belts and climbed out of the flying contraption, she examined him critically. He didn't seem to be injured in the least. In fact, he looked positively chipper in his goggles and brown leather aviator's jacket. All he needed was a white silk scarf around his neck to complete the ensemble of a World War I flying ace.

"Sorry to drop in on you like this," he said, removing his crash helmet and raking his fingers through his straight brown hair. "But this is the only decent stretch of cleared land for twenty miles."

"'Drop in'?" His boyish bravado made her want to administer a good swift kick to his rear end.

"'Drop in'?" she repeated with rising inflection. This man was as mad as a March hare—one of those irresponsible nuts who got a kick out of defying death. And why should she care? It wasn't her problem if this lean, lanky stranger preferred sky diving to quietly watching a sunset.

Her apprehension grew. Just as the small soft mammals of the field scented danger in the wind, her senses prickled. A shudder ran up and down her spine, and her instincts told her to run, to find shelter far away from his laughing dark-eyed gaze.

She glared back at him, meeting his cool disregard with her own steaming indignation. He deserved to be lambasted with the recriminations poised on the tip of her tongue. He should be on his knees kissing the ground after such a narrow escape.

Possibly, she thought all of a sudden, her hostility was misplaced. Maybe he'd received a clunk on the head and wasn't thinking properly. "Are you all right?" she asked.

"Never better. That was one hell of a ride." He removed his leather gloves and strode toward her with bared hand outstretched. "I'm Dane MacGregor."

She yanked off her dirt-encrusted gardening mitt and held out her hand. "Laurel Janeway."

His grasp was warm and enveloping. Long hands, she thought, as befitted a man whose height was well above average. At this close range, she decided that everything about him surpassed the norm, his strong white teeth, lively brown eyes and broad shoulders.

What else would she expect from a man who had swooped down from the skies? Mere mortal traits?

"Are you sure you're not hurt?" she inquired of this superior example of masculinity whose only obvious lack was common sense.

"I'm fine. If you want to worry, think about the plane. I don't know how I'm going to get it out of here." He released her hand and assured her, "I'm one hundred percent A-okay. Except for a little head cold, and I had that when I left Atlanta."

He did sound a little nasal, come to think of it.

"Atlanta, Georgia? You didn't fly that thing all the way from there."

As soon as she spoke, she realized how like a country bumpkin she sounded. Living in mountain seclusion must have erased all semblance of sophistication. Her embarrassment was heightened by his bemused smile.

"Actually," he explained, "the range of this ultralight is only about sixty miles. At least that's what I've been told. This is the first time I've flown in the Rockies."

"Judging from your choice of runway, you're very fortunate that it's not your last."

"I've made tougher landings. This was a piece of cake."

Laurel's jaw clenched. First he scared her half to death with his daredevil tactics. Then he made her sound like a fool for giving a second thought to safety. Even for a pilot, he was carrying the macho, right-stuff thing too far.

"Well, Mr. MacGregor, I was apparently mistaken in thinking that you needed my help. Guess you can take care of yourself from here on in."

She pivoted and stalked toward the burlap sack she'd dropped when she'd heard his approach—his assault—on her meadow. The first drop of rain splattered on the tip of her nose, and she hastened her pace. It would serve him right to be caught in a downpour. A good hard rain might dampen his conceit.

She heard him shout for her to wait and took several more swift strides before she turned. Her affronted dignity was somewhat appeased by the sight of long-legged Dane MacGregor toiling after her up the slope. She usually tried to be more considerate of people who were not used to the altitude, but he deserved to be deflated. There were lessons to be learned about survival up here, and she was inclined to let him struggle with the consequences of his thoughtless bravado.

So many people came into the mountains unprepared, only to discover they were lost without a compass—literally. Or suffering a hypothermic reaction that could have been prevented by a windbreaker and cap. Or caught in the rain, she thought with a grin as she watched him pant and stumble up the steep hill.

Today's weather was a perfect example of nature's whimsy. The sunrise had promised August warmth, but now, by late afternoon, there was a moist chill to the air.

Laurel knew the Rockies were not a comfortable predictable habitat. Human creatures were utterly insignificant and frail against the mountains' rugged serenity. Living in their shadow, she had learned that survival depended on an ability to adapt.

"*Mr.* MacGregor," she said sweetly, "was there something you wanted?"

"Call me Dane," he gasped.

"Certainly, Dane." Knowing he was out of breath, she mischievously prodded him into further conversation. She wanted to underline the fact that he was out of his element. "From your lack of Southern accent, I presume Atlanta is not your original home. Tell me how you ended up there."

"I grew up in the Midwest." He paused for breath. "But I've lived in Atlanta for eight years." Another gasp. "Could I use your phone?"

"I don't have a telephone."

His dark-brown eyes rolled and she laughed out loud at his aghast expression. Her amusement was drowned in a boom of thunder.

She pointed to the northeast. "If you walk in that direction you'll eventually find a graded road. It's twelve miles to the Conifer Lodge, they have all the modern amenities like telephones."

"Twelve miles?"

"That's a walking measurement," she said smugly. From the clouds he might fancy himself master of all he surveyed, but everybody had to come down to earth eventually. "It's considerably less as the crow—or the ultralight—flies."

His measured glance toward his downed aircraft caused her to add nervously, "You're not considering going up in that thing again, are you?"

"Considering," he admitted. "But rejecting. I don't trust the weather."

"I'm shocked. That's the first halfway intelligent thing I've heard you say."

"Do I shock you? Is that why you ran away from me?"

"I didn't run away," she explained impatiently. "I left because you seemed to think you could take care of yourself."

"And you don't think I can?"

"Not without a telephone and a fancy flying machine. This isn't downtown Atlanta, and you can't call a taxi. I think you need my help to get you out of here."

"Maybe." His cool impassive expression made her think he might have some clever plan up his sleeve. "And maybe not."

"I get it," she said. "There's a radio in your plane to signal a ground crew."

"There was," he said. "But it quit."

"On that piece-of-cake landing?"

"Right."

"But you still don't think you need help?"

"I said maybe, didn't I?"

She gave a quick disbelieving snort. This was the most exasperating man she'd ever met. Even if he had zero regard for his own safety and comfort, she couldn't believe anybody would be so callous about the inconvenience he was causing others. "Right this minute," she informed him, "your crew is probably going crazy with worry about you."

"And what do you suggest I do? Stand in the middle of this godforsaken meadow and yell Mayday? I don't even know where I am. Except that there's some ski lodge twelve miles away."

"I didn't say anything about skiing."

"Isn't that what people do in Colorado?"

"Sure. Just like everybody in Georgia lives on a plantation and drinks mint juleps."

He lowered his eyes to his boots and scuffed at a rock. Rather sheepishly, she thought. At least he had the decency to be embarrassed when he'd made a gaffe.

"The Conifer Lodge," she informed him, "is just a motel. Our elevation is only about 7,300 feet, and we're not all that far from Denver—only about fifty miles northeast. On a clear day, if you're standing on top of Saddleback Ridge, you can see all the way to Pike's Peak. But we're not prime skiing territory. Geneva Basin over at Guanella Pass is the closest for downhill, but almost everybody around here does cross-country skiing."

She paused. He was looking directly at her and smiling. It was her turn to be chagrined. She was proud of where she lived, and it took very little provocation to set her off on vivid exclamations over its beauty and attributes.

"I guess," she said, "you're not really interested in a geography lesson. And I do have a suggestion."

"Ready when you are."

"I could use my CB to tell your crew that you're all right. Do you have a handle or call letters?"

"The plane is Red Hawk. And I go by my own name."

"Surprisingly sensible."

Heavy droplets trickled down on them, and Dane climbed to Laurel's level to seek shelter beneath the spreading boughs of a Colorado blue spruce. He turned up the collar of his leather jacket. "Speaking of sensible, isn't there an old wives' tale about not standing under a tree when it's raining?"

"That's not a folk story," she said. "Tall trees like this spruce are often struck by lightning. Of course, we're standing in a forest. The odds are with us."

"Sort of a natural Russian roulette."

"Sort of." She shivered in the wind and rolled down the long sleeves of her flannel shirt. "You're not afraid to take chances, are you?"

"I try not to be."

She wondered how far he would go to prove himself. Where would he set his limit? Beyond the azure skies? Another tremble passed through her. There was a toughness about him. His high cheekbones, prominent cleft chin and thick brow gave him the alert intensity of a predator. But his smile was kind, revealing an innate friendliness in the deep dimples that bracketed his mouth and in the laugh lines around his eyes.

He was a complex man, she thought as she gazed up at him. His dark eyes had a faraway glaze, a look of measured concentration, as though he were reviewing his options. Instinctively Laurel understood that he didn't plan to offer her any apology for his earlier behavior.

Rather than ask for her help or for shelter from the rain, she guessed Dane would choose to succumb to one of the tragic fates of unprepared mountaineers.

It was up to her to make amends, to bend.

"You know, Dane. There's a saying up here in the mountains about people who have narrowly escaped danger."

When he started to protest, she raised her hand to stop him. "I know you don't think you were in any peril, but I suggest you humor me."

"Okay, what's the saying?"

"The good Lord didn't want you, and the Devil wouldn't take you." With a wry grimace she continued, "In light of that, I'd be a mean-spirited woman if I left you to catch pneumonia in the rain. I can't offer a telephone or a sauna, but if you follow me back to my cabin, we can use the CB, and I'll give you a lift to the lodge."

"I have only one question," he said sardonically. "Will your mule carry both of us?"

"Very funny. It's a Jeep." She slung the burlap sack of mushrooms over her shoulder. "Well? Are you coming? Or would you rather wait here for a search party?"

Obstinance shone from his eyes, boring through her. He was clearly someone to be reckoned with, a man who shaped his environment to suit his needs.

She lifted her chin, stubbornly determined herself. Her blue eyes issued a silent warning: *don't expect me to ask again. This tree might bend, but the roots grow deep, and it has never broken.*

"I appreciate your kind offer of hospitality, Laurel." His voice was tinged with sarcasm. "Lead on."

He drew a deep breath and followed her up the gentle incline. His leather-soled boots slipped on rocks covered in lichen as he whacked his way through low-hanging branches.

This trek, in Dane's opinion, was not part of the preferred scenario. This sort of thing never happened to Jimmy Stewart or John Wayne when they were playing pilot.

He'd been scared out of his mind when he'd come in for that impromptu landing, but he thought he'd managed to disguise his fear. Had she guessed? Maybe his handshake had revealed the tremors. Or maybe she'd seen a flicker of panic in his eyes.

In any case, this wasn't working out the way it ought to. All his cool had been for nothing, because Laurel Janeway was clearly unimpressed. Instead of treating him like a conquering prince, she seemed ready to bite his head off. The least she could have done was to throw her arms around his neck, flutter her eyelashes and moan, "My hero."

That would have been nice, he mused as he gasped and struggled to keep up with her. That was how most women would have reacted. Most women wouldn't have schlepped him through the underbrush.

He was glad she'd taken the lead and was therefore unable to watch his awkward progress. Her sure-footed grace made an embarrassing contrast, he thought, glancing up at her pert bottom in the snug-fitting jeans. With the designer label. Why was this mountain gal wearing Calvins?

She was a strange creature, he thought. Full of contradictions. That cornball mountain saying about God and the Devil didn't jibe with her otherwise polished speech. And what was in that sack she was carrying?

Who was she? How did she make her living?

When he had first seen her standing in that meadow, knee-deep in thistles, she seemed to have risen from the earth like Venus born from the sea.

He stumbled on a rock and chastised himself for this lapse into poetic exaggeration. *Get a hold on yourself, Dane. Did you get a look at that unlined face? Those clear blue eyes? You're thirty-four years old, and she's obviously younger. Too young for you.*

A weird sense of disorientation struck him. At this time yesterday he'd been in complete control, issuing final instructions at his advertising agency and promising to be in touch. A mere twenty-four hours later he'd faced the danger of a serious accident and was trudging through parts unknown behind a scampering wood nymph.

But this just might be worth the trouble, he thought, if his first impression of Laurel Janeway proved valid.

While his staff in Atlanta had rejected a score of models who supposedly embodied that "natural look," Dane had discovered the real thing.

A less astute observer might have overlooked her potential; though the baggy flannel shirt, simple braid and lack of makeup created a homely disguise, Dane knew to trust his instincts. He'd been in the advertising game long enough to know what would sell, and the natural look had definite appeal for consumers in their thirties, the latter-day hippies who now lived in split-level, suburban homes. Laurel Janeway radiated health and a straightforward kind of honesty.

His marketing people wouldn't be pleased with his decision. They constantly advised against using nonprofessionals and teased him for his knack of spotting unusual faces in the crowd. The Federico Fellini of advertising, they called him. But they couldn't argue with his success. Hadn't he been the man to engineer a successful marketing program featuring a crochety old lady and the ugliest dog anyone had ever seen?

Not that Laurel was a dog, he quickly amended. He wouldn't have been a man if he hadn't notice her slim thighs and cute, round bottom and those wide blue eyes. But she wasn't a typical model. Too short, for one thing, probably only five foot four. And her nose was pug. Her lips were well-shaped, but thin. And her eyebrows were light and thick.

Still, she had a quality about her that he hadn't seen in the two-dimensional fashion models who paraded through his offices. With mascara on those pale eyelashes and a professional styling for that plaited hair, she could be a knock-out—his latest triumph. Maybe not as big as Cheryl Tiegs, but exactly right for the Meadow Flowers project.

He sneezed loudly and reminded himself that it was still too soon for congratulations. He had to find out more about her and convince her to sign an exclusive contract.

When she paused to retie the laces of her high-topped rubber-soled boots, Dane gasped with relief. Though the climb in the high altitude winded him, he would never have asked her to slow down.

"It's all downhill from here," she reassured him.

"Terrific." Despite the chill in the air, he was sweating.

When she hefted the bag onto her shoulder, he still wasn't recovered and asked a quick question to detain her, "What's in the gunny sack?"

"Wild mushrooms."

"Are they safe? Do you know how to tell the poisonous ones from the nonpoisonous?"

"Of course." She withered him with a mocking glare. "Believe me, Dane, I know my edible fungus. I was a biology major in college."

"College? You don't look older than nineteen."

Her response was a full-throated laugh, head thrown back. Raindrops sieved through the thick evergreen branches to slide down her forehead and catch on her blond eyelashes.

Her laughter was wonderful. Free and rich and full of womanly experience. How could he have mistaken her for a naive young woman? Despite her unwrinkled face and creamy complexion, Laurel's self-assurance proclaimed a wealth of living.

Her laughter subsided, and he wondered. Was she ambitious enough to be successful?

"I take it you're not nineteen," he said.

"You're off by seven years."

"Twenty-six," he said with surprised dismay. That was practically over the hill for a model. He squinted into her face, trying to detect wrinkles that would show up under the camera.

"Don't be so disappointed. You're not exactly an adolescent yourself," she taunted. "I'd guess that you're thirty-six."

"Thirty-four," he growled defensively.

"And a bit touchy about it," she diagnosed. "Well, if you're over your midlife crisis, we really should move on. This is a steep descent, so it's better if you walk sideways."

"I know how to walk down a hill."

"Just be careful," she teased. "We don't want to break any of those arthritic old bones. But let's try to hurry. This rain is going to break like a flood at any moment."

While she side-stepped rocks and a clump of choke-cherries, he slid after her with far less agility. She might have the advantage out here, he thought, but that was a temporary state. Once they were on an equal footing—figuratively and literally—he would test her vaunted maturity against his. He'd misjudged her once, deceived by her seeming innocence, but he'd remember her sly wit. He would not underestimate her again.

Near the base of the hill, he stepped up his pace, not wanting her to turn and find him straggling far behind. The slick leather sole of his boot skidded over a mossy rock, forcing him into a gawky gallop.

She pivoted at the galumphing sound of his descent. Though he managed to control his momentum, he stopped only inches short of a collision with her. His hands went instinctively to her elbows, and she dropped her sack to steady herself against him.

Locked in an embrace, their eyes met. The touch was as unpremeditated as a jagged arrow of lightning, an electric current that flowed from her startled eyes to his. Even more surprising to Dane was the swift change in her expression. In two heartbeats, her astonished gasp became a womanly sigh. He felt her firm, slender body joining with his, closing the scant gap between them.

For the first time in his life, Dane was speechless. He had seen her as a thing, a creature he could mold to his bidding, but she was so much more. Just as her careless clothing hid her potential beauty, her casual manner disguised a vibrant sensuality that challenged and excited him.

He tightened his embrace, sliding his hands around her, caressing the tensile strength of her spine. She was full of life in his arms. What would she be like in bed?

Demanding and strong, he thought, and responsive to his touch. Her skin would be as smooth as satin. Her hair would smell like honeysuckle, and her lips would taste of mint.

Her hands rested on his chest, separating their bodies while she prolonged their eye contact. He saw an intensity in the confident set of her jaw and a hunger in her eyes, evidence of an appetite that he longed to satisfy.

He lowered his mouth nearer to her waiting, parted lips and realized the depth of his need. His desire was more than physical. He wanted to touch the essence of her. With Laurel in his arms, he felt as if he'd captured the wind.

But the mountain winds were capricious, independent and free. Laurel watched his dark eyes as he pulled her closer to him, and her conscious mind warned her against his kiss. She imagined herself standing in the middle of the meadow shouting, "Mayday!" But there would be no rescue from the powerful seduction of her own arousal.

If his mere touch could set her blood churning, what would happen with a kiss? She felt a fluttering sensation in her loins as his thighs pressed against hers. The inside of her mouth was sweet and hot, heated by her accelerated breathing.

An impulse, she thought. Caught off guard by the impact of his lean, hard body, she had reacted without thought or wisdom. Purely natural. Like the rain.

The storm within her gathered force, in rhythm with the downpour. Her pulse beat faster and faster, racing with the rain—from a trickle to a hard, passionate thrum. The fragrance of the forest mingled with his scent in a heady, irresistible bouquet. Even under the sheltering pines, she felt errant raindrops seeping through her thick blond hair. The cool moisture sizzled against her hot skin.

Only a few seconds passed, yet Laurel felt as if she'd gone through an eternity of longing. No matter what else he might do, Dane had affected her profoundly. He'd fallen from the sky to give her this memory, a solace on lonely nights when she would recall the time she'd held a dark handsome stranger.

There could be no more than this unpremeditated embrace. He had to leave before there was a chance for more. She ordered her eyes to stop staring up at him, told her body to cease its yearning. After all, she was mature enough to control her desires and experienced enough to know her own sexuality. Brief encounters, she had learned, were seldom close. There had to be a bond of trust between a man and a woman before there could be satisfaction.

Abruptly she pulled away from him. Her lips drew into a straight no-nonsense line, and her brow furrowed as she brushed back the damp tendrils that had escaped her thick braid.

"I'm sorry, Dane. I should have gone more slowly down the hill."

"Are you?" he asked. "Are you sorry?"

"Yes, we both could have been hurt."

As he watched her pick up her gunny sack and stride through the drizzle, he mentally echoed her warning. Hurt. They could be hurt, but he was willing to undergo the pain for the possible reward.

He wanted her twice. Once for the Meadow Flowers image. And once for himself.

2

THEY HUDDLED beneath the umbrella of trees at the edge of the clearing. Laurel's cabin was only about twenty feet away, but the driving rain made that distance seem a marathon's length.

Her two-story log cabin snuggled among tall spruce and Ponderosa pine at the base of the slope and overlooked another meadow, smaller than the one where his plane had landed.

The window frames of the cabin were painted a dark terra-cotta red. Shielded from the rain by a porch roof were flower boxes filled with yellow and orange geraniums. Details of the three small outbuildings were hazy, but the grounds and a large terraced garden showed scrupulous tidiness.

"Go on inside," she told him, raising her voice to compete with the storm. "The door's unlocked."

"Aren't you coming with me?"

She pointed to a battered, pea-green Jeep Wagoneer that stood several yards away from the house. "I'm going to use the CB to let the search parties know you're okay."

"I'll go with you."

"Why? Are you afraid I might leave you stranded?"

"Afraid?" he scoffed loudly. "No, Laurel, you don't scare me. And let's get one thing straight: I don't take orders from anybody. 'Go inside' sounded like a drill sergeant's command."

She shrugged off his grasp, trying to ignore the tingle of excitement his touch awakened deep within her. This had to be the most inappropriate attraction she'd ever experienced. Dane wasn't the sort of man she would choose. A daredevil without an ounce of common sense? She knew better than that. Her reaction was nothing more than a dumb reflex, the probable result of living alone too long. Why else would her hormones be in such an uproar?

Without another word, she sprinted toward the cabin, tossed her sack of mushrooms onto the porch and dashed through the rain to the Jeep. She climbed inside, flicked the radio to life and made her call.

He joined her, and in an instant the windows were steamed up with the combined moisture of their breathing. Laurel concentrated on the CB rather than the enforced intimacy.

A static reply told her that several CB's were tuned in, waiting for word from search parties.

"This is Laurel Janeway," she said. "The man who was flying Red Hawk is at my cabin."

"Why don't you use my name?" Dane asked.

She flicked the speaker to "off" and spoke to him. "Thanks ever so much, but I am capable of talking on a CB without your assistance."

She answered a question on the radio. "He's all right. No injury, but the plane is a total."

"You don't know that," Dane objected.

The voice over the CB told her to sit tight. Somebody would be there soon to pick him up.

"Do you need directions?" she asked.

Dane took the microphone from her hand. "Hey, Mike? This is Dane. Listen, I'm fine. No need for you to go out in the rain. You wait where you are. The Conifer Lodge? Great, I'll come to you. Ten-four."

He clicked the CB to Off.

Laurel flopped back against the seat, staring through the fogged windshield. "Why did you do that?"

"I was only being considerate. You may find this hard to believe, but these guys probably don't know where you live."

"Anybody around here could tell them. My grandparents built this cabin thirty years ago, and the Janeway family has spent summers and holidays here ever since."

"Are your grandparents here now?"

She shook her head. "They're vacationing in Europe. I'm the only one here full-time this summer."

"Good."

"And what is that supposed to mean?" She whipped her head around. "If you're looking for a little mountain thrill after your crash, forget it. We're already in the car, and we're going straight to the lodge. Do not pass Go, and definitely do not collect anything."

She tromped vigorously on the gas pedal and turned the key in the ignition. The starter chugged and complained before the old engine rumbled to life.

"You leave your keys in the car?" he asked.

"Why not? Nobody in their right mind would steal this heap." She patted the dashboard fondly as if to reassure the Jeep that her criticism shouldn't be taken to heart. "Besides, the first hill out of here is a killer. It takes a running start and lots of skill to make it up and over."

"Is it safe to drive in this rain?"

"No."

To herself Laurel added that it was far safer to attempt the muddy charge over the hill than to spend time with Dane. Her survival instinct warned her that his lanky sexuality could do more damage to her emotional well-being than a broken arm or leg. He was hazardous to her health.

His hand darted to the ignition. He flicked it off and removed the key. "I didn't make it through a plane crash to injure myself by falling off a mountain. I've seen what you refer to as 'little hills.' If it's big enough to worry you, it probably means a sheer drop of over five hundred feet."

"Give me the keys, Dane."

She articulated each word, her voice strangulated with tension. Laurel knew enough about him to realize his goal wasn't road safety. He wanted to get inside her cabin, to turn those sexy eyes on her body and change her mind about an afternoon delight.

"Listen carefully, Dane. I'm not nineteen, as you first presumed. I am not a naive mountain woman, and I don't appreciate the games you're playing. Are you paying attention? Now I don't intent to wrestle with you over my car keys. I will hold out my hand, and you will place the keys in my palm."

Though he accepted her demand and gave up the keys without argument, she saw a mocking defiance in his eyes; he was conceding a minor skirmish in order to win the war. His momentary obedience was without docility, and Laurel feared that she might regret challenging him.

"Thank you," she said. "Please fasten your seat belt."

Her only sensible course was to deliver him quickly to the Conifer Lodge. After that, she would probably never see him again.

Her fingers were tense as she turned the key in the ignition and heard a slow grinding moan. Instead of a rumble, the Jeep barely rolled over. Then it died. Nothing but a click.

Laurel closed her eyes in a wince and tried again.

"Won't do you any good," he cheerfully informed her. "It's flooded. You shouldn't have pumped the gas."

"I know how to run my own car," she snapped.

"Obviously."

"All right," she said, assuming control in the face of potential disaster. "We'll go inside and warm up. The Jeep should be ready to go in ten minutes, and we might as well get out of these wet clothes."

"Exactly what I had in mind."

She flung open the car door and sprinted across the yard to the front porch. Grabbing her sack of mushrooms from the porch, she wiped her muddy boots on a rubber Welcome mat and pushed open the door to a large open room. The dim light of the rainy August afternoon shone through eight latticed windows, highlighting five rocking chairs of various designs, which faced a floor-to-ceiling stone fireplace. There was a horsehair sofa and a dining area and an old-fashioned rolltop desk. The fragrance of spices, herbs and dried flowers perfumed the air.

Laurel hesitated before flicking on the overhead light, muttering half to herself, "The generator has been less than reliable this summer."

At the touch of her finger on the switch, the pine-paneled walls were momentarily bathed in light. Then the electricity flickered and extinguished itself. She gritted her teeth. Everything seemed to be conspiring against her. The last thing she wanted was to be cloistered with him in semidarkness. Quickly she struck a match and lit a kerosene lantern.

She glanced over her shoulder at Dane, who stood framed in the doorway. His lips were parted in a genuine smile emphasized by the deep dimples in his cheeks. "This is beautiful, Laurel. I generally don't expect mountain cabins to be so large."

"There's room for all seven dwarfs," she returned sardonically.

"Would it be all right if I started a fire?"

"We're not going to be here that long."

Despite his size and obvious virility, Dane managed to look like a little boy who'd just lost the big game. "Please, Laurel."

"Go ahead and make yourself comfortable," she grudgingly offered. "I'll be with you in a minute."

Bustling into the large adjoining kitchen, she emptied her sack of mushrooms into the sink and turned on the tap. The cold well water bathed her hands, and she shivered. How idiotic to let him start a fire! It was August. Practical people didn't build fires in August. Of course, this storm wasn't typical weather. She was cold and wet and, truthfully, a fire would feel terrific.

To reassure herself that she hadn't, in fact, taken leave of her senses, she inventoried her kitchen. Natural herbs and spices were arrayed on open shelves beside glass cannisters of stone-ground flour, dried peas and wild rice. There was a place for everything, and Laurel usually performed her kitchen work with smooth economy of motion.

Today she fumbled with the box of wooden matches. It took three strikes and two expletives to light the kerosene lamp. She could hear him in the other room, the polished wood floor creaking beneath his leather boots, and she rested her hands on the edge of the sink, anchoring herself. A gentle warmth spread from the pit of her stomach to her limbs, creating a tingling lassitude all the way to her fingertips and toes.

It wasn't a sensation she wanted or had planned for. A pure animal response. It must be mating season for the Rocky Mountain Laurel, she thought. Or else she'd been drinking too much of the supposedly aphrodisiacal juniper and ginseng tea.

Intimate questions trickled through her mind. How could she explain about the outdoor plumbing? What if he stayed overnight? Was he married?

She became aware of her physical appearance. Why hadn't she worn a bra today? Her hair must look a sight! When was the last time she'd shaved her legs?

His voice, deep and masculine, came from behind her, "Do you have any matches?"

She tossed back her head, jarring loose the cobwebs and realizing that she'd left the water running in the sink. Where was her brain? Water was too precious to leave gushing from the faucet. If only she could turn off her reaction to him as easily.

"A fire won't do any good," she said, tossing him the box of matches. "Not unless we get out of these damp clothes."

"Wonderful idea, but I don't think we wear the same size."

"Don't you worry, Dane. I have plenty of work clothes in different sizes. Male sizes."

When he lifted one eyebrow in a caricature of surprise, Laurel enjoyed his confusion. She decided not to tell him the clothing belonged to her two brothers who visited frequently.

She brushed his arm on her way to the front stairway; his leather jacket was cold and hard. Like the man inside, she thought as she darted up the stairs. He was tough; his reaction to the crash landing proved that. And his takeover of her CB showed that he was aggressive. Still she knew there was more to him than that. If he'd been nothing but a macho pilot, she could have dismissed him with a snap of her fingers. There was something else that attracted her, a well-hidden vulnerability.

In her bedroom, she didn't bother to light a lamp. She slipped out of her wet clothes and replaced them with a floor-length, wool shift, slit high on the side. Before she fastened the last button, she remembered her unshaven legs and changed again—there was nothing seductive about blond stubble. Besides, she didn't want to entice Dane. Or did she?

No, she repeated firmly. He lived in Atlanta, for pity's sake, a city she'd never even visited.

Driving rain pelted her bedroom window, and the thunder roared. Soon, very soon, they had to leave for the Conifer Lodge. The search party would be expecting them.

"So don't get any ideas," she told herself. "You're not destined to be his port in this storm."

She donned her oldest pair of Levi's, put on a bra and pulled a bulky cable-knit sweater over her head. That was as unsexy a costume as she could come up with.

Grabbing a sweatshirt and a large pair of jeans from an oak chiffonier across the hall, she went downstairs.

Dane stood beside the fireplace with one arm resting on the mantel. The fire he had built crackled invitingly, and as he bent to adjust the logs with a poker, she noticed chestnut highlights in his hair. Remembering her resolution to be asexual, she covered her pleasure at this homey picture with gruffness. "For a city boy, you make a pretty good fire."

"You're welcome," he said, reminding her of her manners. "I hated to mask the aromas in this room with smoke from a fire. Even through my stuffed up nose, I can smell something nice. What is it?"

"Wild roses, violets, peppermint. I'm making jars of potpourri." Unceremoniously she tossed him the dry clothes and pointed to the stairs. "You can change up there."

"Potpourri," he said, ignoring her instructions. "What does that do?"

"Nothing. It just sits there and smells good." She fetched a double-topped glass jar from a glassed-in pharmacist's cupboard and handed it to him.

He removed the top, took a sniff and sneezed.

From the same cabinet she took a small clear vial and set it on a table within his reach. "Try this. It might not be as aromatic, but it could be more helpful."

"What is it?"

"An herbal inhaler. It combines the oil of eucalyptus, roseroot, peppermint and a couple of other spices. I harvest everything from the meadows and bogs around here. Except for the eucalyptus, of course."

As he held the vial to his nose and breathed deeply, Laurel couldn't help watching the rise and fall of his broad chest. He'd removed his jacket, and his long-sleeved black knit shirt outlined a lean torso.

"This thing works," he said with surprise.

"It's also effective in a humidifier or when applied as a lotion." She stopped cold, unable to blot out the vision of massaging the pungent oils into his bared chest. "Maybe you'd better get changed."

He held the denim jeans to his waist. The legs ended midway on his calf, and the middle was far too wide. "Not quite my style. When you mentioned the seven dwarfs, I didn't think you meant for me to be Dopey."

"The tailoring isn't important. I just don't want your cold to get worse."

"I'll risk it. My shirt isn't wet at all, and the jeans are only a little damp."

"Suit yourself."

Her eyes were drawn to compare the two pieces of denim. Dane's snug-fitting jeans outlined long muscular

thighs and lean hips. Her older brother, the tallest of the
Janeway clan, was generally recognized as a healthy male
specimen. Next to Dane, he would be short and paunchy.

"How did you learn all this?" he asked.

"All what?"

"This nature lore about herbal inhalers and potpourri.
Is it a hobby?"

"More of a life-style. My father was a schoolteacher—
now he's a principal—and he always had long vacations.
My family spent almost every summer here in this cabin,
and my grandmother felt it was her duty to show us urban brats about nature. We did canning and gathered
herbs and made jellies from chokecherries. I was lucky, I
guess."

"You were. Your home life sounds like *Little House on
the Prairie*, an unusual circumstance in this age of day-
care and broken homes and divorce."

A sharp edge had crept into his voice, and Laurel scru-
tinized his expression. His eyes were bland, almost glazed.
The memory or emotion that caused his bitterness must
be deeply hidden. "Are you divorced, Dane?"

"Never married."

"Me, neither."

"That surprises me. Didn't that all-American wholesome childhood make you anxious to go out and do likewise?"

Again she sensed a harshness in his attitude, as if he
carried a painful grudge. Against what? Or whom? Apparently she was supposed to feel guilty for having a normal healthy upbringing. While she was growing up, her
family had seemed incredibly mundane and average. More
and more often, as an adult, she recognized the precious
oddity of a happy home.

"Come on, Laurel," he teased. "I'd like to hear about the pioneering Janeways. Did you all sit around the fireplace and swap tall tales? Whittling? How about whittling?"

"Not quite. But I do remember a whole summer when my mother and we girls worked on a quilt. Good, clean fun? Hah! I would have killed for a half hour of television."

"Do you have the quilt?"

"No, it's at my parents' house, and it's wonderful—designs about the language of flowers."

"Pardon this question from an urban brat, but I didn't know flowers talked."

"It's a symbolic language. You know, yellow roses stand for jealousy. The magnolia for perseverance. Carnations for love."

A potent silence spanned the distance between them. The crackle of the fire and the throbbing of the rain faded, a rhythmic accompaniment to their unspoken magnetism.

Laurel retreated. She hurried into the kitchen and fired up the propane stove to start the kettle boiling. "As long as we're waiting for the rain to let up, why don't I just put all this herbal knowledge to work. I can make a tea that will knock that cold right out of your system."

He followed her and lounged comfortably against the countertop. He still held the glass container of potpourri, and he read the little tag she'd attached with a lavender ribbon. "'Good Scents.' The calligraphy is very pretty, and the picture is attractively rendered."

"It should be. I was an art major in college."

"Wait a minute. You said before that you were a biology major."

"I was. And an art major. And a lit major. And, for about two weeks, a physical-education major. Some people think that's an indication that I can't make up my mind. But I prefer to think of myself as a Renaissance woman, dabbling in several disciplines."

"And mastering them all," he concluded generously.

"I wouldn't say that. I was positively dismal at women's volleyball."

"And what are you doing here? How did a woman like you end up playing hermit in the mountains?"

"It's a long story," she replied, staring at the teakettle and willing it to boil.

"If this rain keeps up, we might have all night."

"Oh, no," she protested quickly. "I can get the Jeep going. We'll make it up the hill."

"But we still have time for your tea and your story."

"Okay, here's the condensed version. After I graduated from Colorado College—without any marketable major—I was lucky enough to land a wonderful job as an executive secretary for an oil firm, Fierco. They were based in Banff, Canada, with offices in Denver. I had a lot of freedom, since it was basically a one-woman operation. Lots of executives, geologists and salesmen drifted in and out, but no one stayed long."

She paused, editing out her brief love affair with the dynamic president of the company, Alexander Fier.

"I liked my work. I made an excellent salary. I probably would have stayed there forever, but the Denver office was closed down when they expanded operations to Texas."

"Were you offered another position?"

"Sure. I even visited the office in Dallas. But it wasn't the same." A frown wrinkled her forehead. "I would have been working under a supervisor, and my duties would have been cut back to basic typing and filing. I was too accustomed to making decisions and being responsible."

He sniffed again from the herbal inhaler. "Which still doesn't explain what you're doing here."

"Well, I took my generous severance check and my healthy savings account and traveled. In three months I took three tours: New Orleans, San Francisco and a white-water rafting trip. I didn't like the cities much, and the rafting made me homesick for this cabin. I wasn't any closer to making a decision about what to do with the rest of my life. I figured that what I needed was some good old-fashioned peace and quiet. So I came up here. That was eight months ago."

"Are you closer to finding the answers?"

"It's between astronaut and president of Xerox," she said with a self-deprecating grin. "That's the long part to this story—all the things I've considered doing and becoming. Actually, I spend most of my time dabbling with herbs and working in my garden. The soil around the cabin is terrible, and I've had to haul loam for growing. My brothers tease me about it. They say I'm bringing the mountain to Mohammed. Doing things the hard way."

"Has it occurred to you that the same reasoning applies to your career search? Why bother thinking about other life-styles when you're obviously very happy right here?"

"Cruel reality," she said. "My bottomless savings account is running dry. I don't have any way to subsidize my—as you called it—my life-style."

She noticed a slight change in his expression, a shift to intensity. His polite attitude sharpened as though he'd heard the answer to an unspoken question.

Laurel wasn't sure which bothered her more: the fact that his manner changed or the fact that she perceived the difference. After such a brief acquaintance, it seemed odd to be so attuned to his moods.

She shrugged and continued, "I'm down to my reserves of cash. If I can buy a new generator for under two hundred dollars, I can afford to stay here through the winter. There's a farm auction this Sunday in the valley, and I know they have a generator in good shape."

"What happens if someone outbids you?"

"I'll probably stay here, anyway. Last year it was January when I moved in. The generator wasn't reliable then, but I managed okay using the fireplace and kerosene lamps. If I could make a living in the mountains I'd stay here forever."

"That sounds like a decision."

"It's more like a dream," she admitted with a shrug. "One of those what-do-you-want-to-be-when-you-grow-up fantasies, when kids decide they want to be acrobats and opera singers and all sorts of impractical exotic things."

"And what's wrong with those dreams?"

She looked at him; he might have just landed from Mars. "They're not realistic."

"Why not?"

"It never happens. The kids who want to be acrobats discover that heights make them dizzy. And the potential opera singer develops a tin ear. For example, what did you want to be when you grew up?"

"A stock-car driver and a pilot," he said, clenching his rugged hands around an imaginary wheel. "And I'm both."

"Oh, my Lord, you're a race-car driver?"

"Among other things. I've always been able to act out my dreams." Her blue eyes narrowed with skepticism as she regarded the unusual man who stood before her. A race-car driver? She remembered her panic at his forced landing in the meadow and warned herself to be very, very careful. Involvement with him would mean nothing but heartache.

"I've found that for my decisions to become realities, I have to work out the logistics," she said in as sensible a manner as she could muster. "My biggest problem is that I was born in the wrong century. I would have made a great pioneer woman or a homesteader. Unfortunately, the mountains don't provide a complete living anymore. I still need money to buy propane and some of my food and gas for my Jeep."

"And a generator," he added.

"Well, that's a good example. A real pioneer didn't even know what a generator was, but I do. And I'd rather not live without one. If I can't get that generator at the auction, I might have to get practical, find an apartment in Denver and start answering classified ads. Which is not that bad. Maybe I'll get lucky again and find another job I like as much as the one I had at Fierco."

The teakettle whistled to a full boil, and she turned off the burner. "So that's what a nice girl like me is doing in a place like this."

"I can sympathize with almost everything you've said."

She measured tea into a pot and poured the boiling water over it, allowing it to steep. His emphasis on the word "almost" irritated her. "You know, Dane, if I'd wanted an editorial comment on my story, I would have sent it to a newspaper."

"You've got too much spunk to trust your life to luck and the classifieds."

"Thank you, Dane. That will be quite enough."

"You can do anything you want to, Laurel. If you put your mind to it."

"That's a very sound philosophy." And she had heard it ten thousand times before.

"I mean it, Laurel. I haven't even known you for an hour, and I can recognize your potential."

"Is that so?" she muttered. "You and everybody else."

"Who?"

"My mother, my brothers and sisters, my friend, Annie, the guy at the post office, the woman who runs the Conifer Lodge. Everybody. Even Alex."

She halted. The name had slipped out. Alex. She hadn't allowed herself to think about him since their office affair had ended in bleak humiliation. Alexander Fier, president of Fierco, had also talked about her potential—how she could have been beautiful, could have risen to the top levels of management at Fierco, could have been his wife. Laurel had tried to conform to his expectations. She'd forsaken her Windham Hill records for the classical music he preferred, bought new clothes, enrolled in a business-management course. All for nothing. Remembered pain knifed through her, reopening old wounds.

"You all know me so well," she said now. "Why can't anybody accept that I'm content? I'm doing exactly what I want to do. I love this cabin. I love waking up every morning to the chirping of mountain bluebirds and the creek babbling in the meadow. This is my home, and I'm happy here."

"I believe you, Laurel." He held up the glass jar of potpourri and allowed the mellow kerosene light to glisten on it. "Have you ever thought of selling this stuff?"

"I already am selling that stuff."

She inhaled sharply, wishing she could call back her statement. Words seemed to be tumbling out uncontrollably, as if the dam of her reserve had developed several hairline cracks.

Her efforts at selling her homemade products were still embryonic, a dream too special to risk criticism. She hadn't mentioned it to any of her family or close friends, fearing they would take her endeavor to be another stalling technique, another way of avoiding the reality of jobs and mortgages.

"I'm selling potpourris and bath oils and moisturizing lotions in the local gift shop. And herbal teas, of course." She raised her chin defiantly. "Now you can go ahead and laugh."

"Why should I laugh? I think you'll make a real effective entrepreneur."

"I hope so," she surprised herself by saying. "I hope my time and money hold out long enough to give me a chance."

She arranged rye muffins on a ceramic plate. Was it possible that he could be an ally instead of an adversary? She wondered. Maybe she'd become too cautious in her thinking. Maybe he could offer her an unbiased outsider's opinion.

"Thanks for your vote of confidence," she said, setting the plate, the teapot and a jar of honey on a tray. "And here's your reward."

She carried the tray to a small table before the fireplace and served him, adding a spoonful of honey to his tea. "Drink it before it gets cold."

He eyed the mug suspiciously and swirled the pale liquid before asking, "What's in here?"

"A blend of angelica, camomile and comfrey root. Plus other herbs and flowers I gathered in the meadow."

He wrinkled his nose like a kid who'd just been told broccoli is good for him. "Flowers from the meadow?"

"If you were really sick and feverish, I would have added a shot of Grandma Janeway's elixir," she confided. "Made with pure grain alcohol."

"Alcohol?" he said hopefully. "As in wine, beer and Seagrams?"

She nodded and lowered her eyebrows in a mockingly prudish expression. "Strictly for medicinal purposes."

He felt his forehead and uttered a low groan, "I feel a fever coming on. I need a glass of grandma's elixir. On the rocks with a twist of lemon."

"Spoken like a neophyte. Granny's dandelion wine is far more palatable."

He took a taste of the tea and pronounced it good, not great, but not horrid. "I think you're onto something with this herbal-tea business, Laurel. I know this isn't a typical boardroom, but I'd like to offer you a serious proposition."

He leaned forward in his rocking chair, resting his elbows on his knees. The fire cast flickering light over his high cheekbones. Though his posture was relaxed, she sensed a powerful tension in his long lean body.

"Are you incorporated?" he asked.

"If you're an IRS agent in disguise, you can forget it. I haven't exactly made a fortune from my teas and lotions."

"You have filed all the proper licenses, haven't you?"

"Not exactly." That was something she meant to take up with her friend, Annie, who was an attorney. "I know there are permits to be bought and copyrights to be registered—miles of red tape. I wanted to be sure I could handle the manufacturing end of the business. Right now I can pick wild herbs and use the things from my herb garden. But with any sort of demand I would have to start a farming operation, which means buying up land, purchasing equipment and adjusting my recipes."

"Have you done any market tests?"

"Nothing formal, but I am familiar with what's offered in most health stores. There's a vast number of herbal products. Everything I make is there. Of course, there are some differences in the proportions and ingredients."

"That's what I would have expected," he said with a satisfied grin. "It's a marketing and promotion problem."

"I wouldn't exactly call it a problem. There's a limited clientele for herbal products, but I never intended to get rich from this. All I want is to make enough money to allow me to stay in the cabin."

"We can't sell strictly through health-food stores and hope to make any kind of profit, Laurel. We have to go into drug stores and supermarkets."

"'We'?"

"Why not 'we'?" He leaned back in his rocking chair and gazed into the fire. "Meadow Flowers. Do you like the name? Good Scents by Meadow Flowers."

Laurel masked her confusion by taking a bite from a rye muffin. She crossed one leg over the other and straightened the bulky folds of her sweater. Only when she had herself completely under control did she ask in a well-modulated voice, "What in the blue blazes are you talking about?"

"Your new career."

"I don't recall filing an application with you."

"That's the beauty of it. You don't need applications. You don't need classifieds." His voice accelerated as he continued, "You're a lucky woman, Laurel Janeway. The odds against my landing in your meadow were a million to one. But it happened. Congratulations, you've won the lottery. You've been discovered."

"Right." She eyed him suspiciously. "What is it that you do for a living?"

"I own several advertising agencies in major metro areas." He rose to his feet and began pacing the wooden floor, his latent energy burning with more heat than the fire. "How soon can you be packed and ready to go?"

"In a minute."

"Terrific. We'll leave for Atlanta in the morning."

"I said I *can* be packed in a minute. But I won't be. Finish your tea, and I'll drive you to the Conifer Lodge, open the door to my Jeep, shake your hand and probably never see you again."

"Don't you understand, Laurel?" He finished off his tea in one gulp. "I'm offering you a job. All you have to do is write out the recipes for your concoctions."

"That's not the whole picture," she said firmly. "You're not leveling with me."

"You want a scenario? All right. Here are the details. My legal department handles all the necessary licenses and fees. My artists package the product. I supervise the advertising campaign for Meadow Flowers. All you have to do is act as the spokeswoman, pose for print ads and commercials. Maybe—if we're successful—you edit a book with my ghost writers and appear on talk shows."

"And what do you get out of all this?"

"At worst, I get a terrific endorsement for my agencies when Meadow Flowers takes off and becomes the most successful herbal manufacturer in the country. At best, you sign over a percentage of the profit."

"Ah-ha! You want me to sign my life away." She dropped her eyes to study the tea in her mug. "But that's silly. I don't have anything to sign away. I don't even own this cabin. A hundred percent of zero is still nothing."

"Right. It's all to your benefit. After Meadow Flowers is launched, you could have an independent career as a model."

"A model? You think I can be a model?"

He was crazier than she had first thought. Models were willowy and tall with perfect features. Models had fingernails two inches long and could walk gracefully in four-inch heels. Laurel shook her head slowly. "You're still dizzy from your crash landing. I'm no model."

"Sure you are. After we style your hair, pluck your eyebrows and put a little makeup on you, you won't even recognize yourself."

"What if I told you I don't want to change?"

"Every woman wants to be gorgeous." He paused, laying down his trump card, certain of its effect. "Besides, if you play my game you'll make enough money to stay here in your cabin. And to buy a brand-new generator."

"Why should you go to all this trouble for me? You hardly know me."

"That's where you're wrong." He eliminated the space between them in two long strides. His eyes took on the sort of opaque gleam she had seen in stalking bobcats and timber wolves. "I'm an expert. I can tell with one quick glance that you have almost everything I've been looking for, everything I want."

He took a stance over her, bracing himself to conquer any objection she might have. His hands rested on the arms of her rocking chair. "And I've been searching for a long, long time."

Laurel refused to meet his intent gaze. Trapped, she thought. There was no escape. His face was only inches from her own, and she could smell the spicy scent of her tea on his breath.

"I'm going to make you rich and famous, Laurel."

"That sounds like a line from a 1930s movie. And I don't for one minute believe it."

"Perfect! I couldn't market you if you were some wimpy lost waif. You are a woman of today with all the contradictions and complications intact. After a few minor adjustments, every female in America will want to be just like you."

He was overwhelming her. She knew that anything she said would be turned into another asset, another reason for her to go along with his scheme. But what was his scheme? He'd mentioned a game but hadn't told her what constituted winning and losing.

"Why don't you sit over there, Dane? And we can discuss these bizarre plans of yours like normal human beings."

"I like it here. I can see every pore on your face. You have a beautiful complexion. Does that come from one of your special beauty lotions?"

"Maybe, but the state of my skin primarily is due to a healthy life-style. And good heredity." She fidgeted beneath his unrelenting nearness. "Listen, Dane. I can't think with you looming over me. Go sit down."

He lifted her chin with his hand, forcing her to confront him, and her objections faded like waning candlelight. The midnight darkness of his eyes enveloped her. Her past was gone. Her future was nonexistent. For this eternal instant, her vision was limited to the rugged planes of his face.

Her lips parted to receive him, and the gentleness of his kiss sparked fires within her. She was burning with desire. Her mind exploded in scarlet and yellow flames as their kiss deepened.

She felt the mug being taken from her hands, felt herself being brought to her feet. Her body molded against him, creating an unbearable searing hotness, and her arms clung to him with all their strength.

His voice was husky. "Unfasten your braid. I want to see your hair."

Her fingers tangled with the rubber band. "I can't do it. Help me, Dane."

She turned her back to him and felt him tugging at the knot. Through the latticed windows she saw the rain falling in sheets. Yet the downpour failed to dampen her fever. She had never imagined such a heat, this fire in August.

He unfastened the knot and unplaited the thick heavy strands, spreading her honey-blond hair like a mantle. His fingers twisted in the luxurious length, and she smelled the lemon scent of her own special herbal shampoo.

"I knew your hair would be beautiful," he said, the roughness of his voice sending darts of excitement through her. "Like pure perfect silk."

His fingers crept beneath her sweater, encircling her from behind to play across her flat stomach. His touch was cool at first but rapidly absorbed her body heat to become an inseparable part of her pleasure. When he inched his hand into the waistband of her Levi's, her eyes opened wide, and she heard a low animal sound escape her lips.

He stayed behind her, caressing her flesh with brazen intimacy. It was like having an invisible lover who knew the secrets of her pleasure. Yet when he pulled her against his thighs and she felt the hardness of his arousal, she realized her lover had substance and a name.

"Dane," she whispered.

Her hands reached behind her, finding the rough denim of his jeans. Closer, she wanted to pull him closer, to abandon the restrictions of clothing, to join with him.

Beneath her sweater, his fondling strokes climbed her torso. He cupped her breasts and lightly circled the tips with his thumbs, creating a throb of ecstasy.

She felt his lips nuzzling through the thick curtain of her hair, touching the nape of her neck. Alternating shivers of tension and release played along the column of her spine.

It was now or never. She hovered at the point of no return, wanting to trust him, to accept his love making. Yet from deep within her a small voice whispered, "Please, Dane. Stop."

"Not now, Laurel. I want you."

"And I want you," she breathed. "But it's too soon. We have to stop."

"Let me show you how it will be for us in Atlanta. Let me give you a reason to come with me."

Her hands shook as she placed them on top of his and disengaged herself. With one forward stride she was separated from him, and her freedom had never been so lonely. She turned to face him, a confused smile curling her lips. "Isn't that supposed to be my line?"

"What?"

"Isn't it traditional for the woman to offer her body as inducement? Shouldn't I be the one bedding my way to fame and fortune?"

"Thank God for feminism," he replied. "I don't mind using my body to convince you."

She wobbled slightly as she walked away from him, her sense of balance disrupted by the remembrance of his touch. "It would never work, Dane. I'm not a model, and I don't want to be changed. And I don't believe in this scheme of yours."

The farther away from him she went, the more logical her arguments sounded. "Why should you finance my herbal products? We're not talking about a new form of microchip or a car that runs on water instead of gas. I know enough about business to realize that I'm not going to make you a lot of money."

"Don't underestimate me."

Though she refused to look at him, she knew his eyes would be dark, his jaw thrust forward. In the short time she'd known him, he'd conquered her subconscious. Without seeing him, she knew precisely what he was doing.

"I seldom make mistakes," he said. "And I usually get what I want."

"I don't belong in Atlanta."

"Damn it, Laurel." The force in his voice startled her. He spoke with a resonance that would allow no more objections on her part. "Living up here has put you out of touch with reality. I'm offering you the chance of a lifetime, and if you have any common sense, you'd see that."

"Common sense! You're talking to me about sense? A man who drives race cars and crash-lands ultralights?"

"You can make enough money in a couple of months to finance your hermit life-style for years."

"I don't believe it."

"I'll give you a contract."

She stood at the window, staring out at the rain that showed no sign of abating. The scene failed to dispel her confusion. Should she go to Atlanta? So far away from home.

She felt his presence behind her. His heat warmed her, melting her objections. If she was completely honest with herself, Laurel would admit that the most potent argument for relenting was his body. His words would never convince her as thoroughly as his touch.

"Oh, no!" she exclaimed. "Look through the window, Dane."

Two men in yellow rain slickers splashed through the clearing toward her door.

"The search party? I don't get it. I told Mike to wait for me. What's the matter with that guy?" He moved purposefully toward the door. "I guess there's no real harm done. I'll show them that I'm fine, that you haven't abducted me. And I'll send them packing."

"You'll do no such thing," she said.

"I can't leave you now. Not like this."

"A few hours isn't going to make me change my mind, Dane. And that's all it could be. One afternoon."

"Please, Laurel."

"You have to leave." A grim sadness flowed through her as she accepted the inevitability of their separation. The differences between them were insurmountable. "I'd be out of place in your city. And you don't belong here."

There was a sharp rap on the door, and Laurel opened it to welcome the searchers. With a false smile on her face she silently made her farewells to Dane MacGregor.

3

"YOU DON'T BELONG here, Dane."

Six days later Laurel's statement echoed through his mind, and he recognized the truth in her perception. Dane stood in the shadow of a big red barn, watching as the people of the valley gathered for their Sunday auction. Though he had dressed for the occasion in a studded black leather vest, cowboy boots and ten-gallon hat, Dane had never felt more conspicuous.

A stranger, he thought, the man without a name. The romantic drama of that image appealed to the showman in him, and he called up images of classic loners and gunslingers from the movies—*The Magnificent Seven*, *Shane*, all the spaghetti westerns of Clint Eastwood. The corner of his mouth twitched self-mockingly while his dark eyes narrowed in reflex impersonation of the heroic outsider.

He squinted at the cloudless Colorado sky. Was it *High Noon* yet? In the rental car that he'd driven from the Denver airport, he had heard that the high in the Rocky Mountains was in the low eighties, but the dry heat felt refreshing after the humidity of Georgia.

As a cute young thing in tight jeans and a plaid yoked shirt led her sorrel mare past Dane into the barn, he tipped his hat, a gesture that would have been absurd in cosmopolitan Atlanta. She rewarded him with a shy smile, and he hitched his thumbs in his belt. Was he really acting like such a fool? All he needed to complete his cowboy fantasy was a mournful, whistling sound track.

Instead a country-and-western guitar tune twanged over the PA system that had been set up at the auctioneer's table, and an adolescent voice announced, "Ladies and gents, we got about half an hour until the auction. So we're going to make some music to pass the time. You just keep taking your potluck dishes into the community house and listen up."

Dane leaned back against the weathered wood, trying to ignore the way his pointy-toed boots were pinching his feet and musing on the irony of his cross-continent journey. If he'd wanted authentic "country," Georgia and neighboring Alabama offered plenty of opportunity for listening to nasal ballads. Why had he come here?

Because of Laurel. She was becoming an obsession with him. He couldn't forget the delicate fragrance of her thick blond hair. Nor the satiny softness of her skin. The way her blue eyes turned stormy with desire haunted him.

More than her physical characteristics, he remembered her wit and intelligence. Though she managed to embody the earthy qualities of a mountain gal, she was capable of verbal sparring on a sophisticated level. She gave the impression that she would enjoy an evening at the symphony as much as this down-home rendition of "Thank God, I'm a Country Boy."

He couldn't explain the combination of old-fashioned practicality and modern awareness that made Laurel Janeway the perfect image for the Meadow Flowers campaign. Though he'd tried to make his staff understand, they didn't believe him.

Since Tuesday, when he'd returned to his agency full of enthusiasm about Laurel, he'd listened to arguments from his marketing and talent people. They had united in their opposition to his bright idea, using an inexperienced model. No one believed she could be that special. Or that she was worth the time and expense of a complete make-over.

Still Dane persevered in his plans for Laurel. He'd sent three special couriers—two with flowers and one with a contract. She hadn't returned his messages. How could anybody exist in the twentieth century without a telephone?

He'd decided to make one final plea, and this auction was it. As soon as he saw her he'd...he'd what? Beg? Shower her with money? Pull an imaginary six-gun?

There had to be a suitable gesture, but he still wasn't sure what it was. He'd have to count on inspiration.

His fascination with her was irrational, but the idea of never seeing her again awakened a sensation very much like fear. He shifted his feet uncomfortably. What a laugh! Big tough Dane MacGregor—the guy who drove race cars and ultralights—was scared of a little, blue-eyed blonde.

Nobody who knew him would ever believe he could be so affected by a woman. It didn't fit his reputation as a swinging bachelor. Lots of gorgeous females, models and beauty queens, loved to hang on his arm. Women called him on the phone, sent him cute presents, made his bed and cooked his breakfast.

He had his pick. So why was he hung up on a stubborn creature in a flannel shirt? He'd tried to tell himself that he only wanted her as a model. Truly, he couldn't imagine anyone but Laurel for the Meadow Flowers image.

Down deep inside, he knew there was more. She had touched his secret self, his vulnerability. No matter how he accomplished his goal, Dane had to see this infatuation to its natural conclusion. Even if it meant slipping a

Mickey Finn into her herbal tea, he had to bring her back to Atlanta with him.

LAUREL MANEUVERED her wheezing Jeep Wagoneer into the dirt parking lot overlooking the wide field where the people from the valley were gathering for the auction. Beside her on the seat lay her large canvas purse with two heavy brown envelopes inside. One contained two hundred dollars in cash that she'd withdrawn from her savings account to bid on the generator. The other held a five-page contract from MacGregor and Associates, Inc.

The envelopes represented the two choices for her future: buy the generator and stay here; sign the contract and go to Atlanta. Her inclination was to sign the contract.

She hopped out of the Jeep, grabbed her purse and her potluck dish and waited for her friend, Annie Terrance of Denver, to park her Datsun 280Z. Annie had come up for a visit yesterday, and the two women had spent most of the previous night discussing Laurel's options.

When Annie joined her, Laurel stepped carefully down the dirt path from the parking lot toward the community house. Her usual surefootedness was hampered by the strappy sandals she'd worn with her white muslin dress. It was a long time since she'd dressed in anything less practical than boots and jeans, and the light fabric with flower embroidery on the yoke felt wispy and free in the warm summer sun.

Annie, with her short-cropped red curls and freckled nose, looked more outdoorsy in her Levi's, rubber-soled loafers and T-shirt. Without her usual makeup and three-piece suit, Annie didn't seem much like a full-fledged practicing attorney. Yet her earlier advice to Laurel had, for the most part, been sound and intelligent.

"Some things never change," Annie commented. "These auctions and potlucks in the valley are the most incredibly consistent events. I remember when we were ten, stumbling down this same hill behind your parents. What did you bring? Something you were whipping up in the kitchen smelled wonderful."

"Mushroom and pigweed quiche."

"Pigweed? That's disgusting, Laurel."

"But healthy. High in vitamins A and C. It tastes kind of like spinach, but better."

"Do you think Mrs. Jamison brought her chocolate and marshmallow cake?" Annie asked with a wistful sigh.

"Undoubtedly. There hasn't been a gathering in twenty years that hasn't seen that chocaholic nightmare. I've been trying to get her to experiment with carob."

"Don't you dare! Life's pleasures are limited enough."

Laurel winced at an offkey warble from the band. "Mrs. Jamison's son, Lyle, could do with some herbal aid on his vocal cords."

"That's just his voice changing," Annie said. "Even all your concoctions won't provide a cure for adolescence, will they?"

"If I could package that, I'd be a millionaire."

"From the looks of that contract, you might be, anyway."

Laurel stopped short. She didn't want to be rich and famous. Didn't even want to leave the valley. As Annie had pointed out, there was a pleasant consistency to this life. Most of these people had known her since childhood, when her family had spent every summer at the cabin. Their unquestioning acceptance was priceless. Happy memories floated on each gust of wind, and the mountains sheltered her from hurt and confusion.

"Annie? I don't want to go to Atlanta."

"It's your decision."

"I feel so comfortable here. Safe. Are you sure it's a good contract?"

"It's a once-in-a-lifetime opportunity."

Last night they had reviewed the terms in depth. When Laurel had realized that Meadow Flowers already existed as a company, she had felt deceived. Dane hadn't given her that impression. Hadn't he talked about her validity as an entrepreneur?

Of course, she rationalized, there hadn't been time for an in-depth explanation, and the contract clearly stated that her products and recipes would be given special consideration. In the terms, she was referred to as a "consultant," yet her primary responsibilities were as a spokesperson for Meadow Flowers.

"What if I decide I can't represent the company?" she'd asked. "What if I don't approve of their products?"

"That's easily handled," Annie had said. "If Mac-Gregor will accept an escape clause whereby you're free to cancel the contract for any reason."

"I don't know. I really wanted to do my own manufacturing."

"There's nothing in this contract to stop you. I urge you to consider how this offer would increase the probability of your success. Not only are you being offered a handsome salary plus payment of all expenses, but the media exposure is invaluable. Not to mention the convenience. Here's a chance for you to see if the marketplace can stand another herbal manufacturer. Without spending a dime of your own money."

"That's somewhat underhanded, isn't it? Using their money to start my own business, only to possibly be in direct competition one day? Kind of like loving them and leaving them."

"As your attorney, I can only advise you on the legality of your position. According to this contract, you would be within your rights."

"What's your advice as my friend?"

"Don't double-cross Meadow Flowers. You're a terrific person, Laurel. You're my best buddy. But I don't think you've got what it takes to be a scheming businesswoman."

"You make scheming sound like a praiseworthy trait."

Annie had shrugged. "Sometimes complete honesty can be a liability."

Laurel had replayed those words again and again. Perhaps she was naive in that sense. Dane had misled her, but it seemed to be to her advantage to overlook his deception. After all, she stood to gain a comfortable cushion of money. Nothing would be lost except time. His offer surely beat looking for a job.

Still, she didn't like starting their relationship with a lie. And she predicted that the relationship would go deeper than just a business association. She couldn't have been more sure of that than if the terms had been written into the contract. A more intimate association would be implied by a move to Atlanta. Laurel squinted, a sense of déjà vu overcoming her. Some of the parallels could not be overlooked. Dane would be the boss, the owner of MacGregor and Associates. She'd be the employee. Exactly the same disastrous, self-destructive arrangement she'd faced with Alex Fier. Less than a year ago she'd sworn never again to ride that merry-go-round.

She tried to tell herself that Dane was different, that he possessed a fine sensitivity beneath his macho posturing. But honesty once again interfered. She didn't know him that well and couldn't explain why his face appeared in her dreams. Craziness! In the whir of hummingbird wings she imagined the sound of his plane. And she remembered the feel of his hands in her hair.

His special-delivery bouquets hadn't helped to quell her memories, she thought with a smile. Those poor delivery men! They had stood on her cabin doorstep, bewildered by the solitude, their neat uniform caps proclaiming: We Go Anywhere Overnight.

She'd tipped the first delivery man ten dollars when she had read the note attached to the strange-looking arrangement of leaves.

My inhaler is almost empty. Here's a bundle of eucalyptus so you won't have to run off to Australia to harvest. Come to Atlanta instead.

Now she touched the crystal pendant that had been hidden in the second bouquet, a more conventional arrangement of roses and baby's breath. There was another note.

Crystal is the salt of the earth, but I prefer the flowers. Meadow Flowers. I meant what I said. Come to Atlanta.

"Laurel?" Annie called her back to the present. "Is something the matter? You look like a sick calf."

Laurel swallowed and gazed around her. The day seemed brighter than before, fresh-washed and redolent. "I'm going to do it, Annie. I'm going to accept the contract, go to Atlanta, Georgia, and make my fortune."

"All *right*! Then when you're rich and famous you can hire me as your personal attorney."

"I thought you were happy with Lake, Janus and Hunsinger." Laurel paused meaningfully before adding, "Especially with Franklin T. Lake."

"Let's not get started on my own conflicts of interest," Annie replied. Her fair skin blushed in acknowledgement of her special relationship with her senior partner. "Are you still going to buy the generator?"

"Sure. It's a good deal, and I'll need it when I come back to the cabin."

"If—and that's a big if—you come back. From what you've told me about Dane MacGregor, you might just decide to stay in Atlanta." She winked knowingly. "Might be another contract that he offers. A marriage contract."

"Don't be silly. We're too different to be anything more than friends. I could never be serious about a man who does daredevil stunts. It's not like you and Lake. You're both attorneys. You have so much in common."

"This may come as a shock to you, Laurel. But Lake and I don't discuss contract law in the bedroom."

They climbed the rough-hewn steps to the community house and set Laurel's health quiche on a long table where cheese casseroles and platters of fresh garden vegetables were arranged in succulent splendor. Another whole table held gooey desserts. Three huge roasts had been donated by the Bar Q Ranch.

Laurel and Annie chatted their way through the familiar throng and headed for the auctioneer's platform, where the band was acknowledging loud whoops of approval from their high school contemporaries and packing up their guitars.

The grizzled auctioneer, who usually worked behind the counter at the general store, stepped up to the microphone to lay down the ground rules for the auction. "We're talking cash on the barrel head, folks. So you can put away your Mastercard and Visa. This money goes for the volunteer fire brigade, and we aren't taking chances on your credit."

He started his sing-song chant, holding up a hand-operated grape press, then moved quickly through several small items. Laurel was tempted to bid on a butter churn but kept her silence. With exactly two hundred dollars in her purse, she might need every penny to purchase the generator.

Finally it was time. Rather than move the machinery, the auctioneer pointed to the generator and said, "A guaranteed reliable piece of equipment. If it don't work, you can take your complaints out on Lucas Morton's hide. Bidding starts at fifty bucks."

Laurel raised her hand.

"Thank you, Miss Janeway," he said with a broad wink to the crowd. "That little lady hardly looks like she'd know what to do with a generator. Come on, boys. Don't some of you need a fine piece of machinery."

There was spirited bidding in ten-dollar increments up to one hundred forty dollars. Then the other bidders dropped out, shaking their heads. Laurel held the high bid.

"Going once, going twice . . ."

"A hundred and fifty."

Heads turned to see the man who had stepped out of the shadows to make his first offer. The crowd parted as he strode toward the auctioneer's platform.

Dane! Laurel gaped in astonishment. What was he doing here?

Annie tugged at her sleeve and whispered, "Is that him? Is that MacGregor?"

"You bet it is."

"Oh, Laurel. He's gorgeous."

"Right now he's a gorgeous pain in the rear. Why is he trying to outbid me?"

The auctioneer raised his eyebrows and commented, "This dude looks like he's got the cash. One hundred and fifty is the bid."

"One sixty," Laurel snapped.

The auctioneer started his droning—Dane cut him short. One-ninety."

Laurel couldn't believe the irrational arrogance of the man. If he was trying to prove something to her, he'd chosen the worst possible method. She glared in his direction. He was close enough for her to see the challenge in the firm set of his jaw. Why? And why was he wearing that idiotic urban-cowboy outfit?

All eyes focused on her, and she felt a red-hot rage. In a clear hard voice she said, "Two hundred dollars."

"Make it two hundred ten."

She bit her lower lip to keep from shouting at Dane while the auctioneer—and everybody else—waited expectantly for her answer. Laurel shook her head.

The auctioneer's gavel hammered. "Sold for two hundred ten dollars to the gent in the fancy leather vest."

LAUREL WAS TOO ANGRY to stay for the potluck. With her teeth clenched in a snarl, she would never be able to eat Mrs. Jamison's chocolate cake or the Bar Q roasts.

Valerian root was what she mentally prescribed for her state of high nervousness. Or peppermint and camomile tea. She needed something to relax her. Her cheeks were burning, and she could feel coiled stress in her limbs.

The friendly familiar atmosphere at the auction transformed in her mind into a prying crowd. While avoiding Dane, she tried to politely make excuses, to answer the concerned questions of people who'd known her since she was a child.

Working her way toward the parking lot, she whispered to Annie, "I've got to get out of here."

"Running away never solved anything."

"Don't give me platitudes. You saw what he did. I can't believe the ego on that man."

"I also saw how he looked at you."

"For a lawyer you're being awfully romantic. He was trying to manipulate me." She gave a short, humorless laugh. "As if he could control me by buying that dumb generator. Dane MacGregor has the scruples of a weasel."

"And the look of a man in love."

"In love with himself. Listen, I've got to go before I kill something. Are you coming with me?"

"Do you need me?"

"I'd be lousy company. It's probably better if I spend some time alone."

"As long as you're sure about that," Annie said as she checked her wristwatch. "I really need to be heading back to Denver, anyway. Plus I want to sample the potluck goodies before I leave. I'll make your excuses, Laurel. Drive carefully."

Laurel stalked up the path to her Jeep, flicked the ignition and peeled out of the parking lot with a satisfying roar and a cloud of dust.

Damn that man! Her mind was all made up to accept his offer, and he had to pull something like this. Obviously he thought that if he outbid her on the generator she would have no choice but to accept his offer. Obviously she had been misled, thinking sensitivity was his strong suit.

All he had accomplished was to embarrass her in front of the whole valley. And to convince her that she couldn't possibly work with him. As far as Laurel was concerned, he could take a flying leap off the nearest cliff. She didn't need him or his Meadow Flowers contract.

She rammed the Jeep into low gear to make the last hill before her cabin. In a gritty grinding burst of speed, she roared into her yard.

Damn him! She slammed the car door with a fierce metallic crash. Pent-up anger and adrenaline surged through her. She wanted to run, to scream, to kick something.

In wide strides she passed the sunlit shed where batches of fragrant blossoms were soaking and drying inside. She skirted the edge of her garden and picked up the ax. Five trees on her property had been felled by pine-beetle disease, and she had all that wood to split into chunks for the fireplace. Usually she postponed the task but today Laurel was glad to have a way to vent her outrage. She hefted the ax and swung hard.

Twenty minutes later she had a small stack of split pine and an ache in her arms. With each swipe of the ax her anger lessened. Sweat beaded on her forehead, and her white muslin dress was stained with dirt and thick sap.

She pushed the golden curtain of hair from her eyes and stared up through the conifers at the sun. What a mess! A complete disaster!

A trickle of moisture made a path along her dirt-streaked cheek. A tear? She rubbed her face with the back of her hand. She shouldn't be crying. There was nothing to regret. If anything, she should be glad she hadn't accepted his offer. What if she'd been stranded in Atlanta before learning of Dane's overbearing arrogance? She tightened her grip on the ax and took another swing.

"For what it's worth, I'm sorry."

Laurel whirled at the sound of his voice. Before her stood Dane, looking rugged and virile despite his too-new black hat and fancy vest. "How did you get here?"

"Drove. But I left my rental car at the bottom of your hill and walked. I didn't think Hertz would appreciate a bottomed-out axle." He took another step toward her. "Besides, I can run over that hill faster than I could drive, and I thought I might need to beat a hasty retreat."

"You got that right," she said, hefting the ax to her shoulder. "I wouldn't advise you to come any nearer."

"I talked to your friend, Annie. She said you had decided to accept my contract."

"Put that in the past tense and forget it, Dane. If it means working in the same office with you, I wouldn't dream of coming to Atlanta."

"I wish you'd reconsider."

"Why? So you can humiliate me in front of the people down there? Just what did you hope to accomplish by outbidding me on that generator?"

"It was a dumb move, and I'm sorry." He bent to pick up a twig and snap it between his strong fingers. "That's the second time I've apologized in two minutes—I'm more humble today than I've ever been in my life."

Laurel could see the tension in his bunched shoulders, and realized it was difficult for Dane to admit he'd been wrong. But his apology still wasn't enough to appease her. He'd have to crawl across Mt. Evans on his hands and knees to do that.

"Too bad you're wasting all this humility on me. Because I'd just decided that I was lucky. Your tactics at the auction allowed me to see what I would have been getting myself into. I want you off my property now."

He planted his feet slightly apart in a loose, street-fighter's stance and said in a quiet, determined voice, "I'm not going unless you come with me."

"Perhaps you misunderstood. That wasn't a request. It was an order."

"I told you before that I don't take orders from anybody. Let's stop dancing around each other, Laurel. My contract is an excellent offer. Your friend told me you thought so yourself. You're not going to turn me down. Not because you're feeling sorry for yourself."

An immediate protest died on her lips. He was right. She'd been moping, crying like a baby, because her feelings were hurt. Any why should she take his actions personally? Oh, Lord, this was so complicated.

"Let me tell you something," she began. "This isn't the way to get what you want."

"And what exactly do I want?" A glimmer of a smile curved the corner of his lips, and one dimple in his cheek appeared to tease her. Those dimples, more like creases, were so familiar from her dreams. She dipped into the wellspring of her anger, wishing she could see his eyes more clearly beneath the brim of that phoney Stetson.

"I'll start over," she said. "Somewhere in your warped misguided mind you thought you could force me to accept your contract by outbidding me on the generator. Right?"

"I can see how you might think that."

"Which means that you think I'm some kind of helpless dope who can't possibly take care of herself because she's been dumb enough to go through all her savings. Right?"

"Wrong. I think you're brave and strong and self-sufficient. For the third time today I'll apologize. *Mea culpa*. I'm sorry. In my warped misguided way I was trying to give you a graphic illustration of why you should accept my contract. You need money to live up here, and I'm offering you a painless way to earn it."

"Painless?" She remembered her affair with Alex Fier and all the attendant anguish. This situation with Dane was much too familiar. He already haunted her dreams. He was sending her flowers, making manipulative gestures that were insulting. She was crazy to want him. "What you've given me," she said, "is a sneak preview. I have a crystal-clear idea of what it would be like to work for MacGregor and Associates."

"It wouldn't be like that."

"Sure it wouldn't," she said derisively. "I've had some experience in this area."

"You said you enjoyed your job with Fierco."

"The job, yes. But there were...complications with the company president."

"Alexander Fier," he remembered. "An affair?"

"That's right." She lifted her chin, confronting the bitter truth. The episode was not something she took pride in, but he'd asked directly, and she wouldn't lie. "It was a tawdry boss-secretary affair that I was fool enough to mistake for genuine love. Maybe it could have been. But I wasn't able to change into the sort of woman he wanted."

"Was he married?"

"Of course not. I'm not that dumb."

"Then he was the fool to let you go. Don't blame yourself, Laurel. Fier can't be worth it."

That statement was quite perceptive. Alexander Fier wasn't worth the hurt she'd felt. Down deep inside Laurel acknowledged Dane's logic. The loss of her relationship with Alex had been inevitable. He'd made it clear from the start that he was experimenting with her. His demands that she change her basic character were impossible. He wasn't what her parents would call "a good man." Still, she'd loved him, and she couldn't deny the pain.

If there had been anything positive about her affair with Alex Fier, it had been learning to be more careful about giving her trust. She had to consider the consequences. As she looked at Dane in his foolishly endearing cowboy outfit, she remembered that lesson. The similarities between Dane and Alex made her wary.

Her voice dropped to a more calm level. "Why didn't you tell me the truth about Meadow Flowers? When you were here before you made me think I would be the entrepreneur. You didn't say there already was such a company?"

"I didn't lie. You just didn't give me time to explain."

"I don't like being manipulated."

"I promise to handle you with infinite care from now on. Give me a chance, Laurel."

His offer could be taken two ways, and Laurel's mind jumped to the more physical conclusion. She pictured his hands stroking her body, awakening sensual responses, and she looked away from him.

They were supposed to be talking about business agreements, but she couldn't ignore her preoccupation with his body. Not when his shoulders were so broad, and his thighs bulged suggestively in his neat-fitting Levi's.

She pivoted and swung, burying her ax in the trunk of a felled pine. "I'm not going to change. It's taken me too long to find out who I am."

"I wouldn't want you any other way."

"Think again, Dane. I'm stubborn and independent. I don't take directions at all well." She spread her arms wide. "Look at me. Am I what you want in a model?"

"To be honest, you could do with a bath."

Laurel glanced down at her filthy hands and clasped them together, as if hiding her palms could compensate for the layer of dirt, sap and sweat that coated her body and clothing. "See what I mean. I'm not careful about my appearance."

"For someone who's been chopping wood, you look great. Besides, that's why I employ specialists. Mort Joiner will make sure you're perfect before each photograph."

"By any chance, did this Mort person help you select your western wardrobe?"

"He did."

"Then I don't want him within twenty feet of me. If that's his idea of the Wild West, I'd hate to see his notion of glamour."

Dane looked a little chagrined at first, a hint of vulnerability that he quickly masked.

"That's why we need you, Laurel," he admitted. "I knew as soon as I saw the other people at the auction that I was dressed like somebody out of a bad movie. You, however, are an expert. You won't let us make mistakes like this."

"I bet those boots are killing you."

"And the vest is tight, and this hat is sweaty." He yanked off the wide-brimmed black Stetson and tossed it on the woodpile. "You want to know the worst thing about this outfit? It didn't work."

"What was it supposed to do. Make you rope steers and sing like Johnny Cash?"

"It was supposed to impress you."

"To impress me?" She was touched that he'd gone to all that trouble for her, that he dared to be a fool. Yet she couldn't hold back a whoop of laughter as she looked over his outfit. "I sure hope you kept your receipt."

"Would you help me take back this getup?"

Laughter returned a measure of Laurel's self-respect. She wouldn't forget his conceited power play in bidding on the generator, but she could forgive his mistake. Perhaps they had both learned a lesson in tolerance this afternoon.

Despite all her misgivings, she decided to take a chance. She could see the invitation in his dark brown eyes. A challenge? Or a promise? Perhaps both. She needed to discover what was behind his offer. And as Annie had pointed out the night before, the contract could be worded in such a manner that she had nothing to lose. She could always call it quits.

"All right," she said. "We'll talk about Meadow Flowers. After I've had a bath. I don't intend to enter into any kind of negotiation until I feel like a competent clean human being."

THE BATHROOM was just off the kitchen, sharing the same cistern and well-water system. Laurel sighed as she lowered herself into a steaming bath scented with lavender and wild rose. Bathing counted as one of her favorite luxuries, and the decor reflected her indulgence.

Pots of thyme and basil hung in the large uncurtained window, which Laurel always left open, and violets lined the cinnamon-brown tiled sill. Matching tile patterned the wall to waist height, while the upper half was done in creamy wallpaper etched with delicate pale-green herbs. A skylight made the small room appear larger.

She lathered her hair with a homemade shampoo of yucca root, lemon grass and Castile soap and listened to the heavy tattoo of Dane's cowboy boots on the wood floor of the kitchen.

He was pacing, she realized delightedly. There were obvious hygenic reasons for bathing. As well, she hadn't wanted to put herself at a disadvantage in their business discussion by appearing as a ragged scruffy mountaineer. Now she recognized an additional benefit.

Dane was embarrassed. Ever since they'd come into the cabin he had shown signs of agitation. When he had jokingly offered to scrub her back, his deep voice had held a slight catch. He had avoided her eyes as she'd set the tea-kettle to boil and pointed out the canisters of tea and carob cupcakes. And now he was marching on an invisible treadmill.

Laurel submerged in the water to rinse her hair. She would have cut short her bath time, not wishing to be a tease. But Dane's signs of nervousness were too enticing to ignore. If it upset him to think of her lolling in scented water, that was all right with her. After his behavior at the auction, he deserved to be kept waiting.

She turned on the tap in the old claw-foot tub and doubled over to allow the clean water to flow through her hair. The thick dark-blond strands were like silk between her fingers. Wrapping a pink towel around her head, she sank back for a long soak, humming 'The Blue Danube' tune-lessly to herself.

"What's taking so long?" His voice boomed from the kitchen. "What are you doing in there?"

She bent one knee and massaged the length of her slender leg before replying. "Washing my foot."

His response was a low groan, much nearer. "Well, hurry up. We haven't got all day."

"I don't like to rush." Impishly she added, "Bathing is a wonderful natural way to relax. I've scented the water with rosebuds and lavender."

His boot heels beat a retreat, and Laurel chuckled softly to herself. With a loofah sponge she massaged her wrists and elbows. A breeze whispered through the window, and sunlight glittered on a row of glass bottles that held her many herbal concoctions—peach-lotion moisturizer, cucumber astringent and a variety of dried flowers to perfume and soften the bath water.

Laurel leaned her towel-wrapped head against the back of the tub and gazed through the window at the pine forests. Her body felt buoyant and weightless as she trailed her fingers in circles across her abdomen.

She had never felt more desirable. Dane's impatience transformed her average body into a voluptuous marvel. Suddenly there was sensual beauty in the very ordinary crook of her elbow. The memory of his touch flowed through her with liquid pleasure, and her nipples tightened into dark delicate buds. The warm water and occasional tingling winds through the open window sent shivers rippling across her body, and she indulged in a slow feline stretch.

Her mind wandered along the same path as she gazed at the stand of ponderosa pine outside the window. If a tree falls in the forest but no one is around to hear, does it make a sound? Can one hand clap? Her hand pushed through the scented bathwater. If a woman feels desire but does not make love, is she still sexy?

She certainly was. Laurel grinned. The fact that a virile male hovered outside the thin pine door to her bathroom heightened her pleasure, but she did not intend to consummate her desire. Not yet.

A sharp rap shook the door in its frame. Dane growled a question. "Can I come in?"

"Certainly not."

"I could bring in the contract."

"Don't push your luck, Dane. I haven't agreed to sign."

"I'm not the one pushing my luck," he retorted ominously. "Either you come out, or I'm coming in."

The steel edge to his voice told her she'd taken her teasing game to its limit. The desire she'd nurtured in him and in herself bordered on lust. If she continued her seduction, she knew the necessary and probable outcome.

For an instant Laurel considered those consequences. With only a few soft words of assent she might enjoy a pleasurable alternative to tea and contracts. It would be so easy to welcome him into her bath, to make love in fragrant waters.

Not yet, she told herself firmly as she forced the lovely picture to fade. *Remember the auction. Focus on the larger gain.* She should negotiate while she maintained this slight edge. With a deep sigh she rose to her feet and reached for a towel.

"I'll be right out."

She would go to Atlanta, of course, since she couldn't imagine a future that didn't include love-making with this advertising mogul-urban cowboy. The irresistible forces that had been set in motion when he had first touched her would not be denied forever, and this was only a temporary swing of the pendulum in her favor. For now, she would hold herself beyond his grasp, out of touch. It would only sweeten the moment when they would fulfill their fantasies. Soon they would both win.

5

LAUREL SPRAWLED across the double bed in the motel suite that Dane had reserved for her. Though she generally didn't mind traveling, her apprehensions about accepting the MacGregor and Associates contract left her feeling tired and edgy.

She flopped over onto her back. Thus far she'd seen Hartfield International Airport, the inside of a cab and her bedroom, complete with sitting room and kitchenette. Already she hated Atlanta.

The humidity stifled her. She was acclimated to Colorado's dryness, not the sultry South. Air conditioning was an oppressive solution. The coolness seemed filtered and thinned and processed until it bore no resemblance to real air, just as enriched white bread tasted nothing like whole wheat.

And the traffic was loud. And the highway was crowded. And the geraniums decorating the lobby of her motel were plastic. Everything was paved or covered with blacktop. Parking lots. Her glimpse of the downtown skyline showed glass and steel monoliths without warmth or character.

"Complain, complain, complain," she chastised herself. "It's not much different from Denver. Or any other big city."

The difference was in herself. She wasn't visiting Atlanta as a tourist. Nor was she ready to accept this city as her new home. She'd come so that she could make enough money to leave. At least that rationale was what she needed to believe. It would be foolish to expect more from Atlanta. Or from her relationship with Dane.

Far safer to remain detached, to accentuate the negatives. She had difficulty understanding the Southern accent, and though no one was unfriendly, they didn't have to be. Laurel saw herself as a Yankee alien, a foreigner on their hallowed soil, somehow personally responsible for Sherman's March to the Sea and the destruction of their city.

Even the overwhelming green of flourishing trees, flowers and ground cover was depressing, as smothering as a tropical jungle. Shiny-leafed magnolias and cottonwood trees and thick lush gardens only reminded her that this was a different world.

The telephone beside the bed jangled, and she grabbed the receiver. "Hello?"

"Thank God, you're here. I thought you might have had a change of heart."

Unfortunately, she mused, her heart seemed to be doing most of her thinking lately. It maintained an unswerving loyalty to Dane MacGregor and his contract, while her brain had rejected this whole project twenty times.

"I have just one question," she said. "Why did you pick Atlanta for your headquarters?"

"It generally doesn't snow. After living in the Midwest, I've seen enough of the white stuff to last four lifetimes."

He sounded rushed, and she could hear overlapping conversations in the background. Still his voice reverberated through her, setting in motion a surge of anticipation.

She cradled the phone gently, resting the smooth plastic against her cheek. It hadn't even been two days since she'd seen him—certainly not long enough to miss him as much as she did. Their parting at her cabin had been limited to a handshake, and she was anxious to make up for that formal goodbye.

"It doesn't snow in California," she said inconsequentially.

"Laurel, I'd love to chit-chat about the weather, but I'm already responsible for a lot of delays on this project. Can you be ready in a few minutes?"

"No," she protested, sitting bolt upright on the bed. "I need to take a shower and wash my hair and change into something presentable."

"Ten minutes," he said. "A driver will pick you up. As soon as you arrive, join our meeting in progress in suite 1001."

Before she could reply, he rang off. The advantage she'd gained in Colorado was as dead as the telephone receiver.

But that was only right, she told herself. She was being generously paid to represent Meadow Flowers, and Dane was the man who signed the paychecks. The game-playing between them should have been over when she put her signature to his contract and agreed to his terms. Still he didn't have to be so curt.

She leapt from the bed, dismissing her doubts with action. Neither mountain-woman stubbornness nor childish petulance had a place in her immediate future. She was here to learn and to work. To cooperate.

Into the shower and out of the shower in moments, she then flipped open her suitcase. Her least-wrinkled outfit was an unstructured oatmeal-colored jacket that matched a chemise with vertical stripes in tones of brown. She yanked the dress over her head and slipped into the jacket. A wide cinnamon belt cinched the waist. Low-heeled pumps completed the ensemble. Though she'd purchased the dress and jacket only a year ago while working at Fierco Oil, the clothing felt outdated, a former identity dragged from the mothballs.

She also noted a change in her figure since the last time she'd "dressed for success." Though her scale showed a loss of only a few pounds, the outdoor life had firmed and toned her body. Usually that would have been cause for celebration, but Laurel was disappointed with her image.

The beige-and-brown outfit didn't show her figure to its best advantage. The padded shoulders on the jacket made it droop where formerly it had swelled over her curves. She thought she was about as appealing as a scarecrow. And the colors seemed drab, blending with her lightly tanned complexion.

There was a polite rap at the door. An accented voice asked, "Miz Janeway? Are you decent?"

"Just a minute, please."

She pulled a brush through her hair and fastened it at the nape of her neck with a tortoiseshell barrette. Grabbing her huge canvas purse, she flung open the door. "Ready."

A taxi driver's yellow cap in one hand and a wildflower bouquet in the other, Dane greeted her with his teasing Southern gentleman's twang. "Miz Janeway? On behalf of MacGregor and Associates, I welcome you to Atlanta. You were harder than a mule to convince." He dropped the accent and added, "But seeing you here makes it well worth the wait."

"Your hospitality, kind sir, is appreciated." Her calm reply belied the excited thump of her heart as she reached for the bouquet.

He snatched it away. "You Yankee women are so impatient. I left my meeting to deliver these flowers, and I aim to do it right. May I come in?"

"I thought you were sending a driver," she said, standing aside and closing the door behind him.

"How quickly they forget." He went to the kitchenette and rummaged until he found a tall glass pitcher to serve as a vase.

"I drive stock cars. Remember?"

"I certainly do," she said with a shudder.

As he set the flowers on the table beside the pitcher, she studied him curiously. Despite the late-August heat, he was cool and suave in a tailored navy-blue suit. His straight brown hair was combed neatly back off his forehead. Very little of the daredevil pilot was apparent in his manner and attire, even less of the endearing vested dude. He looked like an important executive, someone she'd never met before.

When he turned to face her, Laurel wasn't sure how to act with Dane MacGregor, successful owner of an advertising agency. Should she be the deferential new employee? Or should she remind him of the sexual tension that had permeated their parting in Colorado?

The similarities between this situation and her ill-fated romance with Alexander Fier distressed her. She had tried to banish that ghost. And yet the parallel was too precise to ignore.

Dane's powerful arms were folded across his chest, and his lips quirked into a deep-dimpled smile as he spied her metal footlocker just inside the door.

"I'm shocked," he teased. "I thought you were the type of woman who could travel around the world with nothing more than a backpack, and you've brought a chestful of clothes."

"I beg to differ. That thing—which was a pain to get checked onto the airplane and hauled to the taxi and almost broke the back of the manager of this motel—is full of herbal shampoos, lotions, potpourris and tea."

"We do have those items in Atlanta."

"Not my special blends. I'm more comfortable using my own familiar products. And I figured I might need samples to show to the people from Meadow Flowers. Do you think I should bring something to the meeting?"

"Definitely not. None of the manufacturing people will be there, just my creative staff. And we'll have enough trouble getting through basic introductions with them."

"Why should there by any trouble?"

"Let's just say they don't share my fervor for authenticity. To them, it doesn't matter one whit that you're an expert in all things herbal. They just want a package."

"Isn't that a bit condescending? I'm supposed to be the spokeswoman for these products. Doesn't your staff think the consumer will be able to spot a phoney?"

"They'll come around," he reassured her quickly. "Do you like the motel? It's a bit out of the way from my office downtown, but I thought you'd appreciate the park across the street."

She glanced around the room, noting the plaid wallpaper on one wall and the attractively framed prints of flowers and antebellum mansions. The kitchenette was fully equipped with pots and pans and utensils, and the small round table was maple veneer. An Early American motif carried through in the patterned sofa, coffee table and chair. She was pleased that Dane had taken the trouble to find a comfortable place.

"I like this a lot better than a hotel," she confirmed. "Though the television set worries me. I didn't have a TV in the mountains, and now I'll probably get addicted to dumb reruns."

"Reruns? This is the big city, kid. You've got cable: first-run movies, twenty-four-hour-a-day news or sports from around the world."

"Maybe I can get the management to remove it."

"Not a chance. I plan to be spending some time here, and I need to watch the commercials."

"You're kidding, right?"

"I'm in advertising. I need to keep up on the competition and check out the finished products from my own company. Don't tell me you're not going to be thrilled when you see the first Meadow Flowers spot featuring that natural beauty, Laurel Janeway."

"On television?" She peered nervously at the blank screen, which stared back at her in opaque silence. "I never really thought of that. Me? On television?"

"Locally first. Then we'll go national."

"You mean my parents in Denver are going to see me?"

"Everybody is going to see you. That's the idea. We want to reach as many households as we can."

Though she knew from reading his contract that her likeness would appear in grocery-store displays and magazine ads, actually thinking of herself in television commercials made Laurel queasy. Her preference had always been to project a low profile. Even in family pictures she arranged to stand in the back row.

"Dane, I think we've made a terrible mistake."

"It's not going to hurt. I promise not to let anything or anyone hurt you."

He sounded sincere and warm, but she reminded herself that his business was to create the image of trustworthiness and honesty. His attitude could be a ploy. Yet what would be the purpose of that? It would be bad for his business if she made a fool of herself.

"I hope I don't disappoint you."

"Never. Every time I see you with your long shiny hair and your smooth complexion, I know my decision was right." With a sigh he checked his wristwatch. "I'd like to spend the rest of the day showing you how perfect you are in every sense of the word, but we've got to hurry. And there's one more little matter we need to discuss."

"I'm ready."

"This is nothing earth-shaking for a naturalist like you. Simply a quiz." He picked up his bouquet and separated a woody stalk with heavily drooping sprigs of violet-blue flowers. "Name this plant."

"Wisteria."

"Very good. Here comes the hard part. What does is signify?"

"My grandmother taught me all the flower lore when we made that quilt, but that was a long time ago." She thought for a moment, grateful for this diversion. "Welcome. Wisteria means welcome. Thank you, Dane. That's very sweet."

"I'm not finished." He held up two showy orange-red blossoms. "Come on, herbal expert. What's this?"

"That's easy," she said. "Hibiscus, and it means delicate beauty."

"And these?" He had a handful of lavender-colored stalks.

"The purple lilac stands for budding love," she playfully responded. "I've always thought that was easy to remember, because lilac bushes are as common as infatuations."

"I had no idea a sensible woman like you would have a history of falling in love."

"Often. But usually from afar. I'm sure an advertising person like you is aware of that particular phenomenon.

Isn't that why all those very attractive men are used for packaging and selling products?"

"And all this time I thought women were more intelligent than that. But don't forget, men can worship from afar, too." He plucked another flower from the bouquet and handed it to her. "How about this one? It's not so ordinary."

She took the long sprig from him and inhaled the wonderful fragrance. "Jasmine. Which represents several things, ranging from elegance to sensuality."

"You may guess which meaning is intended. Finally, I have white roses and red carnations."

"Love," she said softly.

They were both quiet as she arranged the flowers in the pitcher. His attentive welcome touched her. Alexander Fier would never have done anything so thoughtful. So there was a difference. Her former lover had never bothered to find out what would give her pleasure, and Dane knew without asking.

With the makeshift vase of fragrant blossoms centered on the round tabletop, her motel suite was transformed into something like home. The suffocating air conditioning took on a soothing quality, and Laurel was glad that she'd decided to come. Dane had made the moment special and alleviated some of her fears.

Still looking at his bouquet, she asked, "How ever did you manage to find all these flowers in bloom? I know Atlanta has a longer and more prolific growing season, but this array is remarkable."

"Didn't you learn anything from that perfect upbringing of yours? Never look a gift horse in the mouth." He drew himself up and proclaimed with mock heroism, "I gathered these posies myself at great personal effort, scouring the streets and byways to create a special gift for you, milady."

"More likely you called a florist."

"Wore my dialing finger to the bone."

"I appreciate the gesture, Dane. It was very thoughtful and beautiful. Before you came in here with your taxi-driver's hat and your bouquet, I'd already decided I hated your city."

"Not homesick already?" He turned her to face him and lifted her chin, trailing a caress along her jawline. "I want you to be comfortable here, Laurel. Whenever you're sad or missing your mountains, I want you to confide in me."

Her hands rose to catch his, and she laced their fingers together. Emotion welled up in her, a feeling of completeness. She squeezed his fingers tightly to keep her tenderness from overflowing.

Her eyes explored the planes of his tanned face above the formal white collar of his shirt and the Windsor knot of his striped silk tie. Such a distinctive face, a face that haunted her whenever they were apart. She happily reacquainted herself with the cleft in his chin, the laugh lines around his dark brown eyes and his high forehead. The creases in his cheeks deepened as he whispered, "I'd like to spend some time with you after the meeting, Laurel."

She nodded, meeting his gaze directly. The wealth of innuendo in his casual invitation was not lost on her. She knew how he wanted to spend time with her, and she was ready.

"I wish we could stay right here," he said wistfully. "But there are people waiting for us."

She drew a heavy sigh and released his hands. Her anticipation had never been greater. "We don't want to be late."

"Besides, we'll have all the time in the world. You're going to be in Atlanta for a long time."

"For as long as it takes," she agreed.

He led her to the door and held it open for her. As she walked into the sultry heat of late afternoon, she heard him say under his breath, "Could take a lifetime."

On the drive to the offices of MacGregor and Associates, Dane entertained her with information about the people she would be working with.

The executive assistant on the Meadow Flowers campaign was Belinda Crawford, a former New York model who had returned home to her family in Atlanta. According to Dane, Belinda could be a powerful ally. She was one of the most self-possessed women he had ever known, able to wither the most vehement opposition with one glare.

Cleo Porter, the caustic copywriter and idea person for the project, represented the major opposition to Laurel, since Cleo would have preferred a professional model for the campaign.

"Cleo?" Laurel asked. "Short for Cleopatra?"

"Sure is. And sometimes this woman is as high-handed as the goddess of the Nile. She even encourages the comparison—she wears elaborate eye makeup and her straight black hair in a blunt cut. But she's the best copywriter in town."

He playfully warned her that Mort Joiner, the man who would be designing her wardrobe, hairstyle and makeup, was in a snit because she had criticized the cowboy outfit he had selected for Dane's Colorado trip.

Finally there was Fred, the photographer, an unflappable pro whose skill with the camera was equalled only by his ego.

"I'll be coordinating the campaign myself," Dane said. "Which makes Meadow Flowers the most important single project for this quarter."

Instead of putting her at ease, his cheerful pronouncements increased her edginess. Despite Dane's light-hearted descriptions, his associates sounded like a formidable group. The high-powered world of advertising was new to her; Laurel was afraid she wouldn't measure up. Her apprehension soared when Dane showed her through immaculate, gorgeously furnished offices and introduced her to Belinda.

Belinda Crawford was tall, pencil thin and intimidatingly beautiful. Hair skinned back in a chignon and skillful makeup emphasized her prominent cheekbones and exotic eyes and displayed her dark skin to advantage. Huge gold hoops dangled from her ears.

Both women watched Dane disappear into the conference room, after which Belinda pulled her aside to offer words of sisterly advice. "I think you've got time for lipstick, honey."

"Aren't we supposed to hurry right in?" Laurel asked. "Dane said the meeting was already in progress."

"Let's get one thing straight. I'm the person who's going to be setting your schedule." She widened her eyes. "Won't hurt anybody in that conference room to wait two minutes."

Laurel dug into her purse to find a fresh tube of peach lipstick. With two quick strokes she outlined her lips.

"What about blush and foundation and eye liner?"

"This is all I brought with me," Laurel said defensively. "I don't usually wear makeup."

Belinda stuck her hands on her hips and shook her head slowly. "Honey, we are in trouble."

"I guess it's obvious that I've never been a model before," Laurel said as butterflies danced a Virginia reel in the pit of her stomach. "I just hope I'll be satisfactory."

"Keep in mind that some people—I won't mention names, but you'll get the picture fast—are never satisfied. As long as you stay cool and calm, there's no problem. You're a real pretty woman, Laurel. Just be cool."

"Ladies?" Dane interrupted. "Anytime you're ready, we're waiting."

Laurel straightened her shoulders and sucked in her breath. Stiff-legged, she marched into the conference room.

There, leafy ferns and rubber trees stood sentinel against white walls decorated with multicolored photos from previous triumphant advertising campaigns. Though the suite was on the tenth floor, the view was predominantly that of other office buildings.

Three other people sat at the table, but Laurel's gaze was drawn to Dane in his sharp navy suit. He was a born leader exuding power and intelligence without being authoritarian, she would bet.

"Ladies and gentlemen," he announced with a showman's flair, "this is our image for Meadow Flowers. Allow me to introduce Laurel Janeway from Colorado."

Belinda gave Laurel a reassuring pat on the arm and took her seat at Dane's left. Hers was the only remotely friendly face. The others ranged in expression from uninterested to outright disgusted.

After a quick round of introductions to Mort, Fred and Cleo, Laurel said, "I'm pleased to meet you all, and I'm sure we'll have a good working relationship."

Mort glared through thick black-rimmed glasses. "Dane told me you didn't approve of his Western look."

"It was a handsome get-up," she replied. "Just not appropriate for the Colorado mountains."

"After seeing your idea of style," he sneered, dismissing her jacket and dress with a sniff, "I don't wonder that you didn't appreciate my selections. A person of your coloring should never wear neutral-colored clothes."

"Thanks for your opinion," Laurel replied, glancing toward Belinda, who gave her a wink.

"Well, it's a professional opinion, luv. I've been in this business for twenty years. What do the rest of you think?"

Before they could answer, a secretary who looked as though she'd stepped from the pages of *Vogue* poked her head into the room. "Sorry to interrupt, Mr. MacGregor. But the Ultra Taste people are on the phone. Do you have time for a lunch tomorrow?"

"I'll take the call." He glanced around the table and with a warning glance at Mort said, "Please continue. I'll be back momentarily."

It was all Laurel could do to keep from grabbing his arm and begging him to stay. The hostility emanating from Cleo Porter alone was palpable enough to knock her off her feet.

"Well," Cleo said, unsheathing her claws as soon as the door closed behind Dane. "Unless we're trying for a sixties hippy look, the hair has got to go."

As Cleo droned through a grocery list of pointed complaints—highlighting lack of makeup and flair—Laurel's frozen smile had cracked. So this was Cleopatra, she thought, as she recalled the fate of Cleo's ancient namesake. Where was an asp when you really needed one?

"Really, guys," Cleo concluded, "no grown woman wears her hair that long. And fastened with a barrette? Is it too late to get another model?"

"I believe your brown eyes have turned sea green," Belinda said archly. "Laurel is an attractive woman. Fresh and natural. Just what we need for Meadow Flowers."

"That's why you're in administrative," Cleo informed her icily, "and I'm in creative."

"Creating trouble, if you ask me."

"Nobody asked, but I'm not wrong. Freddy, what's your opinion? How would you photograph this model?"

Fred glanced up from the Nikon he'd been focusing on Laurel ever since she'd walked into the room. His thick drawl identified him as a native son of the South. "Eyes are a bit close together, but I can make her look pretty. She'll do."

"We're talking more than photos," Cleo said archly. "This woman is going to make personal appearances that can't be retouched in the darkroom. Mort? What's your opinion?"

"She won't work. Like Cleo said, I can dress her for pictures, but she doesn't have the personality to carry off any kind of appearance. She's too short, too."

"Too plain," Cleo added.

"Too blah."

The color was rising in Laurel's cheeks. These snide people were discussing her as if she were a piece of meat—one of the cheap stringy cuts. She pressed her lips tightly together to keep from exploding and tried to think of their sniping as helpful criticism.

"One thing you've got to admit," Belinda said. "Laurel has just the right figure for a model."

"How can you tell that? I can't see a thing under that lumpy-shouldered jacket."

"Quite right," Mort agreed. "Take it off, honey."

"My jacket?"

"You can strip naked for all I care."

Cleo chuckled. "Isn't that the normal state for you back-to-nature types?"

"Hold it right there," Laurel heard herself snap. "I might not be a professional model. I don't know beans about advertising and images. But I am a human being. I'm willing to learn, and I'll work hard to earn your respect. But I insist that we proceed with a measure of common courtesy."

"Terrific," Cleo droned. "She's got a temper."

"Nice color in the cheeks," Freddy said.

"I'll make a note," Mort muttered. "She gets all red faced when angry. We'll have to avoid orange tones."

"Stop it. I have a name, and I would appreciate it if you would direct your comments to me."

"Laurel?" Cleo asked sarcastically. "Or would you rather be Miss Janeway?"

"Laurel is fine."

"Then listen to me, Laurel." Her name sounded like an expletive rolling off Cleo's tongue. "From what I understand, Laurel, you've spent your life romping in some mountain meadow, talking to the animals. Well, this is the real world, Laurel. And it's hard, and it's cruel. You've got to be tough to make it, Laurel. We're professionals, and we don't have time to pamper some little mountain tootsie, even if the boss thinks you're hot stuff."

"Talking to the animals, as you put it, has given me some background for dealing with you, Cleo. Frankly, I'd rather spend time with a rattlesnake."

"What a quaint comparison! You must be no end of amusement for Dane."

"Exactly what are you implying?"

Dane strode back into the conference room. He rubbed his hands together and said, "We have a lunch tomorrow with Meadow Flowers. We need concepts, people. Have you made any progress?"

In the coolest voice she could muster Laurel replied, "We've just been getting to know each other."

"That's good." He noted Laurel's angry blush and Cleo's preoccupation with the papers on the table before her. "At least I think that's good."

"A very important process," Laurel confirmed. "Now I know just where I stand."

"Then let's move ahead. I want a direction for this campaign. Cleo, what are your ideas?"

"Sorry, Dane. I've come up with a zero."

"Maybe this will help. Laurel is more than a model. She's also highly knowledgeable about herbal products. Didn't you have some questions about the ingredients in some of the products?"

Cleo sorted through a stack of notes and found a yellow legal pad. "Let's start with shampoo. Has she had a chance to try the lemon-grass fragrance?"

"I haven't used any of the Meadow Flowers products," Laurel replied. "So I can't really offer an opinion."

Cleo threw down her pencil in disgust, and Belinda tried to explain, "She's not looking for an endorsement, honey. Just tell us something about this lemon grass."

"It's indigenous to southern Asia, I believe. And used in shampoo to cleanse and give luster to your hair."

"Swell," Cleo said, making a note. "Anything more original? I mean there are a million products that claim to make your hair shiny and clean. We want to know what's different about all this herbal junk."

"In the first place," Laurel said, "it's not junk. Herbal substances are distilled from living growing plants. They provide natural remedies, representing age-old traditions of medicine often more valid than modern chemistry."

"How about some one-line descriptions? Like 'natural.' And 'healthful.' And 'safe.'"

"I couldn't say all herbs are safe. Belladonna and foxglove are also herbs."

"Well, we're not trying to poison anybody. What we want is the magic reason that will cause Hannah Homemaker to choose our brand name."

"Maybe we could focus on the flowers," Fred put in laconically.

"What flowers?" Cleo asked.

Dane shifted his weight uncomfortably from one foot to the other. "The Meadow Flowers people have been sending over various samples of wildflowers."

"I've seen them," Mort said. "Real cute. They're all tagged with their old-fashioned meanings. You know, white roses for love. Orange blossoms for purity."

"Narcissus for egotism," Laurel put in with a pointed glare at Dane. "Yellow rose for treachery."

"I thought that was jealousy," Mort corrected.

"Close enough."

She felt Dane's hand on her arm and took a step away from him, refusing to meet his gaze. If there was apology in his eyes, she didn't want to see it. As far as she was concerned, he'd gone over to the side of the enemy.

The remembered fragrance of his wildflower bouquet turned bittersweet. He hadn't made a special effort to please her. He'd simply grabbed the nearest advertising tool and dashed out the door. Like his promises to protect her, the gesture seemed empty.

She listened to him interact with his professionals as they discussed the most appealing bottle shape and the most seductive colors for the package. This hadn't been what she'd expected.

Laurel wanted Meadow Flowers to represent an alternative for the consumer, a chance to use pure natural products without investing the time to harvest and dry the herbs. Her goal was to help people, to make life a little bit more satisfying.

These people seemed to think selling was all a con game, tricking the customer into buying their product. They used words like "lure" and "tantalize." Though Dane contributed little to their discussion, Laurel was disappointed in him. Why was he even listening to someone as vicious as Cleo Porter? How could he have described her as the best copywriter in Atlanta?

Very quietly Laurel added her two cents. "Once people have had a chance to try a truly natural product, I'm sure they'll be smart enough to judge for themselves."

Her comment left silence in its wake, and she continued, "Have you tried the shampoo, Cleo?"

"No, but if anyone else asks me, I'll swear I use nothing else."

"Maybe that's why you can't come up with a concept. Either a Meadow Flowers product is a sham with a token trace of herbs, or it's better than the other products on the market."

"It doesn't really matter," Cleo told her. "Our job is to sell the stuff, not to market-test it. Don't be so naive, Laurel. There are heaps of outstanding products that fall by the wayside because they haven't been properly promoted."

"That's right," Mort backed her up. "It doesn't take much to build a better mousetrap. What's tough is to get people to buy it."

Laurel gently refuted them. "I can't completely believe that. If people are offered a valid choice, I think they'll find what they want and forget the rest."

"I can't believe this," Cleo groaned. "Really, Dane. Do we have to listen to the model?"

"Yes." His voice was terse and hard, and Laurel could see the tension in the set of his jaw. "As I told you before, she's not just a model, but an expert in this field."

"Give me a break. She's a face and a body. That's all she's contracted to be. And I'll tell you right now that I am not thrilled with your choice, Dane. I think your little mountain mama leaves much to be desired."

"That will be enough, Cleo."

"I will have my say," she protested. "I don't see why we're stuck with a dumb blonde simply because you took a trip to Colorado and got the hots for her. It's not fair to the whole campaign to hire your new woman friend."

"You're fired, Cleo."

His ominous words hung over the long meeting table. Almost imperceptibly Mort and Freddy adjusted their posture away from Cleo, who was gasping like a fish suddenly thrown out of her familiar waters.

"You can't mean that," she said. "I've been with you for three years."

"I won't tolerate your attitude, and I despise your false accusations." Dane's anger transformed him into a frigid businessman far more frightening than an outraged blustering man would have been. "For three years you've made valuable contributions to our projects, but this time you've overstepped. You seem to have forgotten one very important detail: I am the owner of this agency. My decisions are the ones that count."

"You're right, Dane. And I'm sorry. It won't happen again."

Cleo's dark eyes glittered with unshed tears. Laurel could only guess at the humiliation caused by her admission. Of course, Dane was right. The woman had gone too far.

Mort cleared his throat, taking a stand that Laurel suspected was courageous for him. "I think you should reconsider, Dane. Cleo's one of the best creative talents in town. Besides, we're a team. We work well together."

"He's right," Freddy added. "I don't want to break in a new copywriter."

Dane massaged his chin with his hand, intently searching each face before he spoke. "I'm sure any other agency in town would be happy to welcome each of you. Singly or as a team. But my most important immediate project is Meadow Flowers, and none of you seems to be even marginally aware of the concept. Laurel was right when she said the consumer would appreciate the quality of these products."

All eyes turned to Laurel, and she once again felt like an outsider, a foreigner who had blundered into their world. Because of her association with Dane, she'd screwed up the lives and careers of these people. As distasteful as she found them, Laurel experienced pangs of guilt. She had no right to interfere. They were experienced professionals, and she seldom paid attention to advertising—much less created the glossy images that promoted a new product on the market.

She couldn't allow Dane to dismiss his staff, not even to assuage her own hurt feelings. The problem with the Meadow Flowers project, she knew, was not the creative failure of these people. It was her presence. They resented her.

"I have a solution," she offered.

Dane fixed her with his gaze. Behind the mask of hard leadership she saw a glimmer of vulnerability in his eyes. Yet his voice was cold. "Keep out of this, Laurel."

"I can't. This is partially my fault. I can't allow you to dismiss these people."

"It's not your concern."

"But it is. I have thoughts and feelings and beliefs that won't let me sit idly by while you make an irreparable mistake."

"Your sensitivity is misplaced. I'll handle this situation in the way I think is best."

"Aren't I allowed to disagree? Do you think, like Cleo, that I'm nothing more than a face to be photographed?"

"Of course not."

"Then sit down and listen. I am the problem with the Meadow Flowers campaign. Cleo doesn't like the way I comb my hair. Mort despises my taste in clothing. And Freddy couldn't care less about who or what he's photographing. As was pointed out, your creative staff is professionally qualified to make those kinds of judgments. I'm not. I'm just an average woman with feelings and emotions."

She glanced at Belinda, whose sympathetic nod encouraged her. "I want to thank you, Belinda, for your kindness."

"Honey, I was a model for years. A piece of goods. I can't count the times I wanted to say what you're saying."

"I think you all know what's coming next," Laurel said. "I quit."

She turned on her heel and stalked from the conference room.

6

WHEN SHE WALKED OUT Laurel didn't slam the door. She closed it carefully with a very considerate but final click.

The sound plummeted dismally through Dane like a silver dollar tossed into a deep wishing well. He waited long seconds for the splash, and then it hit him. She was gone.

A chill wracked his body as he braced himself to accept her decision. He'd come so close. In her motel room she had been on the verge of trusting him. She'd almost admitted she cared for him. Her body had been primed to his touch. And he'd chosen to leave, to end that moment.

His gaze raked the conference room. This meeting, this supposedly creative conference with his staff had destroyed his chance for a relationship. He'd given up Laurel for the shape of a shampoo bottle.

His palms were sweating. Every detail in the conference room leaped into painfully sharp focus—a yellow pencil on the table, the blue black of Cleo's hair, the nubby weave of the neutral thermal drapes. The chic tidiness disgusted him. The conditioned air offended him.

"Belinda," he said in a clear voice that sounded to him as loud as gunfire. "Go with her. Tell her I want to talk."

"I'm on my way."

When she touched his arm to comfort him, Dane almost flinched. The pressure of her slender hand felt like a ponderous weight. It took an effort for him to hear her voice. "That is one fine woman, Dane. I won't let her leave town without seeing you first."

"Very good." He turned to the three still sitting around the table. He cleared his throat, adjusted his necktie and slipped into the utterly cool controlled voice of an executive. "Now where were we?"

He knew they wouldn't perceive the painful regret that cowered within him. No one ever suspected his inner doubts and fears. In his sky diving and piloting and racing, people were awed by the calm self-possessed manner he affected.

He was expert at packaging the invincible Dane MacGregor, a man's man who was irresistible to women. The role was so perfectly acted that at times he believed it himself. Except for the nights. When he was all alone in his oak-paneled study with his display of winner's trophies, plaques and ribbons, he noticed tarnish on the brass, and the image of himself that he'd constructed crumbled.

"Lady and gentlemen," he said, "I demand your apologies or your resignations. Which will it be? Cleo?"

"I was out of line," she said tersely.

"Thank you. Since you find it difficult to accept my choices and decisions on Meadow Flowers, I am reassigning you to Bell Homes and Construction."

"Will I have to write classifieds?"

"Probably. We handle all media and print advertising for Lawrence Bell. Plus brochures."

"Brochures," she groaned. "I don't think I can stand that. Do you have any idea how many gushy descriptions of septic systems and storm windows I've written? Please, Dane, give me another shot on Meadow Flowers."

"I don't see how I can. If I can't convince Laurel to come back, I'll be looking for someone very much like her to represent the products. And that type of woman seems to offend you."

"My career," she said with a bleak mixture of pride and sorrow, "is my life. I promise you will get my most professional effort."

"I'll take that into consideration." Dane turned to the other two men at the table and raised an eyebrow.

"I'm sorry," Mort said quickly. "And I want to stay on Meadow Flowers."

"That's fine. Let's have your input, Fred."

"Get her back, Dane." The photographer tapped the lens of his camera. "I got her last speech on film, and my instincts tell me she's going to be terrific. Maybe not a hot prospect, but warm. Definitely warm."

"Develop those pictures," Dane instructed as he headed out the door. "I'll be in my office, but I don't want to be disturbed. I'll see you people first thing tomorrow morning. And I want some viable concepts before lunch."

AN HOUR LATER Dane spread the black-and-white proof sheets on the desk before him. Freddy had chosen to blow up one shot to eight by ten size—a full-face shot of Laurel. The anger in the thrust of her jaw contrasted with the gentle curve of her cheek. Her pale eyes glittered, and the highlights in her hair made it gleam like a crown.

Freddy's instincts had been right: Laurel was dynamic on film. She projected a sincerity and appeal that would sway the most cynical consumer. Her charisma was truly an advertising man's dream.

As he stared at the photo, Dane's thoughts were not concentrated on promotion. His thumb traced the oval of her face, and he whispered, "Stay with me, Laurel. I've never wanted a woman so much. I don't deserve to be trusted, but trust me."

He checked his wristwatch for the umpteenth time. What was taking Belinda so long? Why hadn't she called?

He considered alternatives. Since it was after five o'clock, Belinda might have assumed he'd left the office. Maybe he should go home to wait. But what if she called while he was in transit?

Helpless, he thought. Important, life-changing events were taking place, and he was helpless to affect their outcome.

The phone on his desk jangled, and he grabbed the receiver. "Belinda?"

"It's me, Laurel. But Belinda is right here if you want to talk to her."

"Where are you? When can I see you again?" A shiver passed through him. What if she was calling to say goodbye? What if she didn't want to meet him face to face? More aggressively he repeated, "Where are you?"

"At Kandy's, a little restaurant on Peach Tree and—"

"I know where it is. I'll be there in a minute."

"Would you please wait, Dane. I have something I need to tell you first."

"Yes?" He closed his eyes against expected pain. Instead the silence continued for several seconds. "Yes, Laurel. What is it?"

"Drive carefully," she said.

"I will." He replaced the receiver on the hook. His hand still rested on the telephone, as if he was unwilling to sever contact with her.

LAUREL SPUN AWAY from the public telephone at the entrance to Kandy's restaurant. She was jubilant. She felt like dancing; so preoccupied with her private joy that she almost tripped over a waitress as she returned to the table for two where Belinda sat waiting.

"I ordered for you," Belinda said, obviously amused by Laurel's dippy aura of happiness. "I take it your conversation was all you hoped it would be."

"He wants to see me," Laurel confided brightly. "And that's enough for now. I was afraid he'd hang up on me after the way I screwed up his Meadow Flowers program."

"I know you're not dumb, Laurel. So you must be blind. Can't you see how much that man cares for you?"

"So you've told me. Back in Colorado, my friend, Annie, said the same thing. Do you know what I think? You're both an illustration of the Ling-Ling principle."

"The what?"

"Ling-Ling is the giant panda given to the United States by China. Zookeepers all over the country tried for years to get Ling-Ling to mate. They couldn't stand to see that female panda sitting there unattached."

Belinda rolled her big eyes and said, "You think you and Dane are like a couple of pandas?"

"In a way. There's something about unmated men and women that makes people want to match them up. Hence, blind dates and matchmakers and Ling-Ling's zookeepers."

"Honey, sometimes you carry the naturalist bit too far."

"Sometimes," she admitted with a grin. "Did you say you'd ordered for us?"

"Sure did. Crab, oysters, wild rice with honey, mushrooms and artichoke hearts. And two kinds of wine."

Laurel laughed. "That sounds like a love feast. All those things are natural aphrodisiacs."

"When you get to be an ancient thirty-five-year old lady like me, you learn not to leave anything to chance. And since this is a dinner for two, I intend to make myself scarce."

She rose from the table and gave Laurel a wink. "My guess is that I'm going to be working with you on Meadow Flowers. But if you and Dane come up with a more private arrangement, too, good luck. Keep in touch, honey."

Laurel watched as Belinda gracefully moved through the dimly-lit restaurant, turned and winked again. "A more private arrangement." How nicely that phrase put everything into perspective!

Laurel had realized—as soon as she walked out of the conference room—why she had really come to Atlanta. It wasn't to become a media star or to make a million dollars or to embark on a career as an herbal entrepreneur.

Strange as it seemed, she'd left the mountains to explore her own subconscious and discover the potential for a relationship with Dane. Since the first time he'd touched her Laurel had known they were destined to cross uncharted terrain together. It seemed a simple and obvious conclusion, yet her brain had been working overtime to dismiss this fascination for him.

Laurel prided herself on her innate truthfulness. She was a straight shooter, direct and quick. Why wasn't she acting that way then? That was partly Dane's fault. If he'd confronted her honestly with his desire, she might have been more able to understand her own yearnings for him. Instead he'd drawn up contracts and urged her into an unsuitable profession. She almost laughed out loud. *Her* face on television commercials? Her body reclining across the staple in foldout magazine ads? The fact that she'd gone along with him indicated either a desire beyond reason or an incredible stupidity.

A private arrangement was exactly what she wanted, a chance to go with her instincts. Thankfully she had that chance. She'd almost told him on the phone that she loved him, but that was premature. And far too important an announcement to be made from afar.

She wanted to love him, but as yet she wasn't sure of her feelings. All she could promise was a willingness to try. Tonight, she thought. Tonight she would let down the barriers and forget the past. Tonight she fully expected to consummate their attraction after an ambrosial dinner.

WHEN HE ENTERED THE RESTAURANT romantic violins seemed to play an overture in her head. He was so smooth and handsome, the sort of man who compelled immediate deference from waiters and the maître d'. Pride swelled in her as he walked toward the table.

He took the seat across from her. Without a word, their hands met. His dark eyes had never shone so clearly, she thought. She was giddy with anticipated delight.

"Laurel," he said. "You're so lovely."

"Dane." Her lips twitched in a smile.

"What's so funny?"

"I'm just bubbling over. Wait until you see what Belinda ordered us for dinner."

The wine steward appeared at their table, and Dane hurried through the ritual tasting and sniffing of the cork. After the steward had half filled their wineglasses and disappeared, Dane proposed a toast. "To you, Laurel. Your beauty, your health and your happiness."

They clinked glasses, and she took a long sip. "My turn. To Dane MacGregor, the man who fell from the sky."

He held the stemmed glass to his lips and drank without taking his gaze from her face. "This isn't what I expected," he said. "I thought I'd be in for an argument. Or at least a prolonged discussion of why you should trust me."

"I don't want to argue. But we do need to clear the air. Trust is a good place to start."

"What can I say? I'm sorry as hell about that scene in the office. Not more than twenty minutes after I promised you that I wouldn't let anyone hurt you, Cleo released her venom."

"This isn't about Cleo. And it certainly isn't about protection," she scoffed. "I'm not a delicate hothouse plant that needs to be fussed over and coddled. I'm a grown-up woman who should be able to take care of herself. I don't blame you for the rudeness of your staff."

She paused. "Trust is the point, Dane. Honesty between you and me."

"Us?"

"That's right. We were kidding ourselves to believe I could be repackaged as a model. The contract I signed with MacGregor and Associates was a bad joke."

"No," he said abruptly. "I was right about you. Freddy snapped some candids at the meeting, and you have presence. You come across well on film."

"Stop right there." Her voice was low and firm. "We are not going to digress. We're going to talk about real things. Real emotions."

"Fair enough." He settled back in his chair and folded his arms across his chest. "The ability to deal with reality isn't one of my finer traits, but I'm willing to try."

"The issue," she said, "is why I signed your contract. My true feelings. I didn't come to Atlanta to be the Meadow Flowers lady. I came because I wanted to be with you."

Dane's mouth gaped open, then snapped shut, but surprise still registered in his eyes. She studied him, waiting for further reaction. Her cards were laid on the table, and she felt good about her plain speaking. This was the closest she'd ever come to propositioning a man, but she wasn't embarrassed.

"Do you still feel like that?" he asked. "After what happened today?"

"One thing bothers me," she admitted, setting her wineglass on the table and running her finger absently around the rim. "The wildflowers. You shouldn't have led me to believe they were something special just for me."

"They were," he protested.

"Somehow I have the feeling you have bouquets by the gross for convenient distribution."

"Not true. I don't know any other woman who would appreciate wisteria and lilac. Laurel, I don't know anyone else like you."

"Are you complaining or complimenting?"

"A bit of both." He seemed to overcome an inner struggle, speaking finally in a quiet tone that impressed her with its depth and sincerity. "I'm sorry, Laurel. I guess I'm so used to hype that it's hard for me to be honest. But I'll try."

"So will I."

Their salad, featuring artichoke hearts, avocado and watercress in a raspberry-vinegar dressing, arrived. Laurel immediately picked up her fork and took a bite, proclaiming it delicious.

The main course of king-crab legs and wild rice with honey was equally satisfying. As Laurel cracked the segmented shell and slowly drew out the sweet meat, she explained to Dane why she wasn't a vegetarian. "I like meat, and I love fish. Once I tried being a strict vegetarian. That lasted about two months. Then I found myself at a hamburger stand scarfing up about four of the greasy little things and totally disrupting my system."

"Don't tell me which hamburger place," he teased. "One of my biggest clients is a fast-food chain."

"Anyway, I decided I probably wasn't getting enough protein from my vegetarian diet. It's smarter for me to just listen to my body. When I want meat, I must need it."

"It's nice to know I don't have to limit myself to nuts and berries when I'm in your company."

She dipped the succulent crab meat in melted butter and bit off a chunk. Her taste buds tingled in ecstasy. Nothing gave more purely sensual pleasure than eating. She glanced across the table at Dane, licked the butter from her lips and smiled. Almost nothing.

"Do you realize," she said, "that our menu is almost completely composed of aphrodisiacal foods."

"I didn't realize. But I approve."

"Which reminds me, don't drink too much of the wine. After three glasses it tends to diminish rather than encourage."

"Diminish and encourage what?"

"Appetite," she said slyly.

Dessert was chocolate mousse. It was almost too much. Laurel was full but couldn't resist a spoonful. "I shouldn't eat this," she said. "Sugar makes me crazy."

"Laurel, may I be serious for a moment?"

"As long as you're not going to lecture me on sugar. I know how awful it is. I think it's criminal the way cereal companies seduce children."

"When you walked out this afternoon, I felt . . . I don't know exactly how to explain it.

"I wish you'd try. . . ."

"It was like the moment before I crash-landed the ultralight, like the instant on a track when I can feel the wheels sliding out of control."

"You've never crashed a race car, have you?" she asked in a small quiet voice as she plunged her spoon back into the parfait glass and folded her hands to keep them from trembling.

"They're stock cars, Laurel, and I've come close."

"Why do you do those things? Flying and driving and risking your life. It's terrible."

"There's a thrill to those sports. And a sense of accomplishment when the challenge is over. The speed and the altitude are exhilarating."

"You can go fast doing something sane, like downhill skiing," she said, and then corrected herself. "Forget I mentioned that. You'd probably insist on ski jumping or finding some other crazy way to make the sport dangerous."

"Partly it's the danger that excites me," he admitted. "But I didn't want to talk about this. I was trying to find a way to explain how I felt when you left."

"When you put it in those terms, I'd say the word to describe your reaction was relief."

"Nothing could be further from my mind." He toyed with his wineglass, finally lifting it to his mouth and draining the last sip. "It was fear, Laurel. I was scared."

She was very still, trying to make sense of all the messages he was sending. It must have been hard for Dane to admit his fear, and she wanted to be gentle. "I don't quite understand."

"I was afraid of losing you."

"I know what you mean—" she hesitated "—there's always that risk. In any relationship. Maybe it's best, in the beginning, not to think of the future."

"Now I don't understand.

"I'll be blunt. Barring natural disaster, we're going to make love tonight. That much is inevitable, but there is no way we can predict what will come after that."

She touched the corners of her lips with her white linen napkin and placed it on the table. That was blunt, all right. And risky. She'd just played her honesty to the hilt. What if he didn't feel the same way? What if she'd read the signs all wrong? She hesitated for an instant before confronting him with a direct challenging gaze.

"Shall we go?" he asked with a broad smile. "To accept the inevitable . . . ?"

7

THE FIRST THING Laurel saw when she walked into her motel suite was his bouquet of wildflowers. They represented so many different moods of their relationship—thoughfulness, disillusionment, desire and fear. "Even if you did just grab the nearest flowers on your way out of the office," she said, "it's a wonderful bouquet."

"Those are just posies. You. You are wonderful," he said, closing the door and fastening the lock. "Your hair, your eyes. The way you move. Everything about you." He rested his hands on her waist and gazed down into her face. "It's funny. I've waited so long for this moment, and now I'm hesitant."

"And I'll bet I know why," she teased, unable to suppress a happy chuckle. "There's always an uncomfortable moment between a man and a woman when he's wondering: does she or doesn't she?"

"What?"

"Take birth-control pills." She grinned and confided, "I don't."

"Laurel, I assure you that—you don't?"

"I tried them once, but all those chemicals didn't agree with me." His shocked expression encouraged her. "Of course, there are natural methods—juniper-berry tea and millet taken daily. There's the ever-popular wild yam, and the Cahuilla Indians recommended a tea of poverty weed."

"You're kidding, aren't you?"

"Am I? There really are an amazing number of ancient herbal preventatives—a fact I always find fascinating, since our generation thinks it has invented something new and different."

"Yes, indeed. Deep down we're no different from the Cahuilla Indians. Seriously, Laurel, are you really set on this type of experimentation?"

"Alas," she moaned, posturing dramatically, "this natural woman you see before you is a sham. Not only am I not a true vegetarian, but I admit to using modern technology, practical preparations for an ancient pleasure," she purred. "Are you still hesitant?"

"You have managed to throw me a bit off balance."

"Then allow me to provide some encouragement...."

She slid her hands over his shirtfront and clasped them behind his neck. With steady pressure she pulled him close enough for a delicate kiss.

"How's that?" she whispered. "Feeling better?"

"Much better...."

Their second kiss was lingering and deep, exploring the promise of Laurel's dreams. She had known they would be like this together. It was inevitable that they would race toward uncompromising delight. Her heartbeat went from a quiet thumping to a crescendo. She felt as if she was running hard, yet anxious to increase the pace even more. She tasted him greedily, her tongue sliding over his smooth white teeth and plunging beyond, deeper.

Dane's strong arms crushed her against him, and she groaned, increasingly impatient to feel his warm flesh.

"Am I hurting you?" he asked.

"If this is pain, hurt me some more."

"I knew it," he said with a laugh. "Beneath the calm exterior of that sweet, old-fashioned girl lurks the soul of a nymphomaniac."

"Talk is cheap, MacGregor." She ran a teasing finger up his jawline to tickle his ear.

Past the sofa and television, past the kitchenette, they fled into the bedroom. By the time Dane had turned on the bedside lamp and yanked back the covers, she had stripped off her jacket and wriggled her sheath dress up and over her head.

"Hold on," he protested. "I'm supposed to do that."

She slithered out of her lacy white slip and pointed to her bra and panties. "I saved the essentials for you."

"Laurel, this isn't a race." But now there was a twinkle in his eyes too.

"Haven't you heard?" she asked, crossing the room in swift strides and peeling off his suit coat. "It's always better the second time around."

"I was looking forward to enjoying the first."

"And so you shall." She had loosened his tie and was working her way down his shirt buttons in quick deft motions. "Why do men wear so many clothes?"

"To protect them from women like you." His shirt and tie were gone. As she unbuckled his belt he grasped her busy hands. "Laurel? You're not shucking corn, you know. There is such a thing as finesse."

She backed away and placed her hands on her slim hips. "You do the pants. And the shoes and socks."

With his back to her, Dane sat on the edge of the bed and slowly untied one shoe, then the other. Humming to himself, he dawdled over each sock, rolling them into neat little balls and placing them in his shoes.

Laurel clenched and unclenched her fists. The interplay of muscles in his shoulders fueled her excitement. Her loins throbbed. She was ready to explode with desire. "Dane? Can't you hurry?"

"Do you remember that bath you took in the mountains? The tune you were humming while I was going berserk in the hallway outside? I think it was 'The Blue Danube.'"

"So that's our problem," she said. "You're stuck on 'The Blue Danube,' and I'm already into the *William Tell* Overture." She paced the short distance at the foot of the bed. It must be mating season, she thought, for she had never experienced such a depth of need. She wanted him—immensely, happily, completely. There seemed to be nothing else in the world except them. He and she and an all-consuming desire.

"I won't wait another second," she announced.

Pouncing like a hungry lioness, she leaped across the bed and threw her arms around his neck. She was overjoyed, laughing, unable to check the flood of her passion.

Her fingernails drew rough circles through the hair on his chest, and he shivered against her. "You're a tease," she whispered into his ear.

"What about you?" He swung his body and encircled her in an embrace. "I suppose your routine in the bath wasn't teasing."

"That was different. I'm an herbal tease."

He groaned at the pun that occurred to him. "Herbal teas?"

"A natural woman." She smiled hugely, gazing up into his shining dark eyes. How on earth had she waited this long? He must be the most sensual wonderful man she'd ever seen. "With natural appetites and desires."

"Laurel, you're amazing."

"Take off your pants," she growled.

They scrambled around on the bed, unhooking his belt, fumbling with the zipper and tugging at the fabric of his trousers. Finally he lay before her, naked and very, very aroused.

The time for hesitation was over. The apprehension she'd felt when she'd first seen him, piloting his cherry-red ultralight and crashing into her life, had been transformed into intense eagerness. Tremors prickled through her.

His hands found the catch on her bra and unfastened it quickly, untangling the straps from her arms as he pulled her to him. Their flesh met, hot and moist and complete. Laurel groaned with heightened anticipation. It had never been like this for her before. Her need for him was powerful and fierce, but not at all frightening. Natural, she thought, like the elements. The rest of her life had been becalmed, and now she was caught up in the force of a typhoon.

While they were still clasped together he slid her white bikini panties down her long slender legs. She was breathing heavily, panting as she held out her arms. When he molded his body to hers, a tingling pleasure passed through her. Her thighs parted immediately to welcome him. Her arms tightened around him convulsively. "Now, Dane."

They joined smoothly, her body the perfect sheath for his. Thrust after thrust drove them to climax. She twined her legs with his, matching his rhythm and urging him harder... until she went rigid. The muscles in her groin contracted in fluttering spasms, and she felt the pure ecstasy of release. Floating on pink fleecy clouds, she listened for a moment to the sound of an ocean's surf, though they were nowhere near a shore. A wide satisfied smile curled her lips.

"Dane, that was... heaven."

He eased off her as they kissed tenderly, after which she snuggled in the crook of his arm. Her tangled hair spread damply around her head and shoulders.

She opened her eyes and gazed down the length of his body, openly admiring his lean well-muscled torso and the endlessly long legs sprawled on the cream-colored cotton sheets. He wasn't a hairy man, and she was glad of that. Dane's sprinkle of soft dark hair tapering to a thin line was almost artistic, perfect in Laurel's estimation.

She traced the tan line just below his navel and said, "Let me guess how you got that tan. From doing something insane and dangerous. I know, during the summer you do flagpole sitting. Act as shark bait? Wrestle alligators?"

He caught her hand and carried it to his lips. "I have a friend with a yacht in Florida."

"A male friend? Or female?" She glanced into his dark brown eyes, then quickly looked away. "I'm sorry, you don't have to answer that."

"A male friend. You have every right to ask me anything. This, my darling, is not a one-night stand." He propped himself up on one elbow to look down on her face. "I mean that, Laurel. I won't let you leave me. Not now."

"Aren't you forgetting something? I quit this afternoon. I can't stay in Atlanta without a job."

"The position of spokesperson for Meadow Flowers is still open, and I want you to fill it."

Laurel wrinkled her nose and tugged at the bed clothing, dragging the top sheet across her body in a semblance of modesty that seemed absurd now that she and Dane were lovers. They always seemed to be talking business in the most inappropriate postures.

"From what I saw this afternoon," she began, "I don't know. Although there were a couple of things in the advertising process that fascinated me."

"Is that so?" he asked sardonically. "You gave an excellent impression of someone who was disgusted."

"All right. I'll tell the whole truth and nothing but." She laid a slender finger on his nose. "It was you. You fascinated me. You looked so powerful and in control in your tailored suit. I liked watching you in action."

"Just goes to show you. Appearances can be deceiving."

"What does that mean?"

"It's all a front. A lie."

She would have laughed at the absurdity of the comment, but something about his expression told her he was serious. "I don't like to think you're a liar."

"I don't, either. And I'll try not to be." He rolled back on the bed, staring up at the ceiling. "Keep in mind that even now I might not be telling you the truth."

She imagined a funhouse mirror in which Dane was reflected and reflected into an infinity of images until it was impossible to tell the real man from his reflection. "Why?"

"I'm not sure anymore. I've been doing this all my life, trying to be who other people expect me to be. Maybe that's why I'm good at advertising. I can sense what people want and give it to them."

"What about you? What do you want?"

"Right now?" He focused on her. "I want you, Laurel. Come back to the office with me tomorrow."

"I don't see how I can. I'd like to work with you. And Belinda is terrific. But I meant what I said earlier about cynicism and advertising."

His eyes, she thought, were deeply vulnerable, almost pleading. She wanted to make him happy, but she couldn't ignore her own feelings. "I'm sorry, Dane."

"I want you back. Nothing else matters."

"That's very nice in theory, but you can't be with me to hold my hand every minute. Nor would I want you to." Laurel adjusted the sheet over her breasts. "Cleo and Mort despise me, and who knows what Freddy is thinking."

"Freddy took some excellent candid shots of you today. He not only likes you, he told me to get you back. Forget about Cleo and Mort. I'll take them off this project."

"But they're the best. You told me so yourself."

"You are the best," he whispered, nuzzling her ear. His hand slipped beneath the sheet to find her belly and begin a slow massage. "What was that you said about the second time around?"

"I can't recall anything but a smart comment about the *William Tell* Overture."

"Well, watch out, lady. The Lone Ranger is ready to ride again."

He lowered his mouth to hers for a tantalizing leisurely kiss, and she threw aside the thin cotton sheet that separated them. The gentle friction of their bodies and the spreading warmth of contact melted her resolve. He slowly withdrew. Hovering above her, he said, "Don't leave me."

She knew why she would stay. It wasn't for advertising or a great salary or to prove that she could do it. Laurel had to remain in Atlanta for Dane, for the relationship between them. Only a fool would turn her back and walk away.

"I'll be here," she said. "For as long as it takes."

"Let's take longer this time. . . ."

His finger traced her lips, the firm line of her chin. He lightly kissed her eyelids.

"Dane?" she said suddenly. "Let's take a bath."

"Is this your less-than-subtle way of telling me that my twelve-hour deodorant has lost its effectiveness?"

"Of course not. I love the musky way you smell." She slid from his grasp and scampered to the foot locker in the front room where her herbal potions and lotions were stored.

An exasperated shout echoed down the hall. "Laurel! Get back here!"

"You'll love this," she promised as she found the bottle containing rose water, tincture of musk and ambergris, a subtly evocative fragrance used since ancient times as a restorative aphrodisiac. She also grabbed a bottle of honey.

She paused at the foot of the bed, gazing fondly at the confused face of her lover. "Think of this as a market test for Meadow Flowers. This erotic bath should be made available to everybody. Everybody over twenty-one, that is."

She started steamy water running and glanced around the motel bathroom, displeased with the sanitary white decor. When Dane appeared in the doorway, she asked, "Would you please fetch the flowers from the table?"

After more rearranging, the bathroom was transformed into a suitably exotic setting. The commode held Dane's wildflower bouquet. Homemade scented candles glowed from their votive holders. Laurel doused the overhead light and pinned her hair on top of her head with the tortoiseshell clasp.

Taking Dane by the hand, she led him into the tub. Their bodies were lit by flickering glow, and the heady fragrances perfumed the moist air. They knelt in the hot relaxing water. Her taut breasts grazed his chest. Gently he kissed her. In the candlelight she could see his smile and the dimples creasing his cheeks.

"What happens now, herbal tease? This tub is a mite small for the two of us."

"Hmm." She smiled back. "I guess you'll have to be creative."

"I kind of hoped you'd say that."

Using the buoyancy of the water he uncurled her legs, straddling them. The position was unexpected, and she raised her eyebrows. "This is never going to work."

"Quiet. This is my fantasy." He unfastened the tortoise-shell barrette and spread her long golden hair around her shoulders. "You look like a mermaid. All slick and shimmery in candlelight."

She leaned back, bracing herself on one elbow. Her other hand reached out to stroke his cheek. She was virtually immobile from the waist down, and the gentle confinement enhanced her excitement. As he gazed down on her with dark delicious promises in his eyes, a tingling spread from her loins to every sensitized part of her body.

Her voice was thick and husky. "A mermaid?"

"And I've caught you."

His hands took her firmly by the waist, lifting her against him and arching her back. As his arm slid behind her, supporting her weight, his lips found hers. Their kiss was deep and probing, mingling the wetness with their tongues. Laurel felt her mind going blank as she sank into a dazed state of purest pleasure.

She seemed to hear the rush of a mountain river, roaring inexorably toward the sea. The current flowed around and through her, as if she had become a part of the churning white water. While Dane slowly, tantalizingly stroked and fondled her breasts, she surrendered to the thundering ecstasy of his touch.

"Beautiful," he murmured. "Beautiful Laurel."

She could only moan in reply, unable to speak. Yet her body was singing in harmony with the rushing river. Wordless thrumming, unstoppable currents.

A blanket of steam kept them warm, and their flesh met and separated, giving them slippery tactile delight. He kissed the line of her throat. His fingers played lightly upon her breasts and down her torso. She felt his hardness against the juncture of her thighs.

With liquid grace he reversed their positions. She was astride him, floating free in rose-scented waters.

His hands directed her pelvis. The raging torrents within her stilled, and she experienced a sweet, gentle peace as she glided toward her destiny. Soft currents parted her legs, and he lowered her onto his hardness. Slowly they stroked together, setting the hot waters into a rhythmic turbulence, swirling Laurel and Dane in whirlpools of desire.

When they had found their mutual satisfaction, she collapsed against him.

"You're right," he rasped. "This is an incredible product."

"I wonder if it would work for everybody."

"Who cares? I'll order the whole supply for my personal use. I'm going to corner the market on rose water. And on you."

"A selfish thought," she teased. "But very appealing."

When they'd risen from their bath and toweled each other dry, Dane whispered, "I hope you're not tired."

"I always find a bath refreshing." She held up the jar of honey and added, "Use your imagination."

He settled her on the bed, gazing at her body with unconcealed pleasure. "You're remarkable, Laurel. Every beautiful part of you."

She squirmed under his compliment, already beginning to feel renewed arousal.

Dipping his finger into the honey, he sweetened her lips. "Don't lick it off," he said. "That's my job."

"You're the boss."

"Now where else . . . ?" He painted twin daubs on her breasts and set the jar aside, eager to taste the combination of her creamy skin and honey. After a teasing lick that set her quivering, he nibbled lightly. "Delicious," he murmured.

Her honeyed lips welcomed him as they shared the sweetness.

He drew away and reached for the jar. "I'm going to coat your entire body," he said. "Starting right here."

Dragging a honey-laden finger along the inside of her right thigh, he carefully drew a secret mark with the pure thick syrup. His tongue and lips found the golden dollop and slowly savored it.

Laurel tried to hold herself still, but the tingling sensations had become unbearably intense. She writhed on the bedsheets, clutching the pillow behind her head until she thought she couldn't stand any more.

"Dane," she gasped hoarsely, "that's enough."

Their pace was furious as he entered her with the ferocity she demanded, culminating in an ecstasy so complete that it left her limp.

"You've taught me something tonight," he said quietly as they cuddled under the covers. His voice sounded faraway and peaceful. "And I thought I knew everything there was to know about the birds and the bees. . . ."

"Obviously," she murmured, "you have a natural aptitude for this sort of lesson."

She felt utterly relaxed. The tension that had been coiling within her had sprung. Was this some sort of trap? If it was, Laurel didn't care. She was content to savor the splendid eternal moment of pure satisfaction.

With a gentle sigh she whispered, "I think I'm going to like Atlanta."

8

A MUCH DIFFERENT Laurel Janeway breezed into the offices of MacGregor and Associates Advertising the next day. In place of her ill-fitting suit dress she wore a flowered dirndl skirt and a pastel-blue muslin blouse with full sleeves and a peplum waist. Her pumps had given way to comfortable sandals, and her long blond hair hung loosely around her shoulders.

A fresh aura of confidence radiated from her, reflected in the healthy pink glow of her cheeks, the azure eyes that were sparkling and clear and the satisfied smile arching her slightly swollen lips.

Belinda gave a long low whistle as she regarded the new Laurel. "I hope you notice, honey, that I'm not asking questions about last night."

"Good. Then you won't hear any lies."

"No, ma'am. You don't have to say one word. 'Course I knew before you got here that last night went just the way I figured it would."

"And how do you come by this clairvoyance?"

"Simple observation," Belinda said. "I was sitting in Mr. Dane MacGregor's office, taking notes on the Meadow Flowers project, and he stopped talking. Just quit in the middle of a sentence like there was something more important on his mind. So I looked up and saw this big powerful advertising exec picking petals off a white daisy."

Laurel giggled as Belinda pantomimed the ritual of "she loves me, she loves me not," with exaggerated joy at the former and utter desolation at the latter.

"When he finished," Belinda continued, "it was for sure on a 'she loves me,' because he just sat there grinning like a bear with his paw in the honey pot."

Belinda's unintentionally appropriate comparison sent Laurel into gales of laughter. That silly little story gratified her almost as much as Dane's whispered reassurances of the night before. If Dane was crazy enough to pick petals off flowers like a schoolboy, he must be completely besotted. Just as she was. Her intuition was confirmed, she thought with another happy chuckle. Last night had been special.

"Who's making all that noise?" Mort Joiner whined as he marched up to Belinda's desk.

"This place needs a little ruckus," Laurel told him, gesturing to the tonal beige walls and the subtle decor. "It's so manila."

"'Ruckus' is a quaint word for it, but I do agree. High tech is fashionable but bland. Of course, I wasn't consulted on the interior decorating."

Laurel kept herself from speculating on the possible result of Mort's ideas of chic. All she said was "Too bad."

"Well, let's get busy." He rubbed his hands together and glanced at Belinda. "She's a bit late, isn't she?"

"We're not going anywhere, Mort—" Laurel took him by the shoulders "—not until we get one thing straightened out." In a firm voice she set the ground rules. "My name is Laurel. When you have a question about me, I'm the one who will answer it. Not Belinda. Not Dane. Not the lamppost on the corner."

"All right. Laurel, aren't you coming in awfully late?"

"How could I be late? You didn't even know if I'd be here at all." She released him. "What time would you suggest I be here in the morning?"

"Depends on your schedule, of course. For today and possibly tomorrow we'll be doing the make over on you, and I want to start early. About eight-thirty?"

"Eight-thirty it is. Now we're ready to get busy with whatever it is you're going to do."

She followed Mort to a one-room beauty parlor with two chrome adjustable chairs facing a wall of mirrors. Though the predominant tone was white, Mort had added bright touches to his private domain, a rainbow-colored kite that hung from the ceiling, a red coat rack and yellow director's chairs. Laurel studied a grouping of photographs on one wall and asked, "Were these all taken in New York?"

"My sister sends them. They're not artistic. I don't know why I bother to hang them up."

"Maybe you miss the place," Laurel suggested. "Or the people."

"Miss it? New York City? Are you whacko? It's nothing but cold drizzle in the winter and heat in the summer. Muggers on the subways. Crowds. Noise."

Mort's wistful expression reminded Laurel of a lover denying the special madness of his first affair. He ran a hand over the thin strands of black hair that inadequately covered his scalp.

"It's a decaying, dirty old town," he finished. "Take a seat, Laurel."

"What are you going to do?"

"Trim that mane. I'll keep the length, but cut it in layers. And it has to be much shorter around your face. Then maybe a perm." He picked up a pair of scissors and made snipping motions in the air. "Definitely a perm. We'll try for tendrils around your face, emphasizing your mouth and chin line."

"We'll try no such thing. I don't want my hair cut. Nor will I agree to a permanent. I tried one many years ago, and my hair is too thick to hold it."

"That's why I need to trim it."

He waved his scissors, and Laurel grabbed a can of hairspray to defend herself.

"Don't be difficult, Laurel. You'll love the results."

"You keep away from me with those scissors. You're almost bald. You've forgotten how long it takes to grow out somebody else's mistakes."

"There's no need to be nasty about it."

"I'm sorry." Laurel set down the hairspray. "Could we start with something else? Something a bit less drastic?"

"Makeup?"

"Fine." Laurel took her seat before the huge mirror and asked, "Is Cleo still working on this project?"

"Who knows? She's been cloistered with Dane in his office for half an hour. Would you mind if I wrap your precious hair in a towel so it doesn't get in the way of the makeup?"

"Of course not."

As Mort brushed the flaxen curtain of hair back from her face, Laurel watched him carefully in the mirror. Maybe he was right. Maybe she should let him clip her hair into a stylish mass of tendrils. After all, he was a professional, and it had been months since she'd even glanced through a fashion magazine.

She wished Dane would join them. He wouldn't want her hair cut. From the first time they'd met he'd admired her hair.

Her reflection in the mirror stared back at her as her hair was wrapped and pinned under a white-towel turban.

Mort was explaining how he planned to use makeup to create the illusion of a perfect face. He would raise the cheekbones, soften the jaw and widen the eyes. In his description, her features were disembodied things, waiting for the magical touch of mascara wands and rouge to come to life.

As Mort instructed her to close her eyes and began to apply foundation, Laurel wondered again about Dane's opinion. Of course, he had ordered the make over, hadn't he?

She watched curiously as Mort applied highlight and shadow in broad bold strokes. Though he blended taupe and tan and peach into delicate shadings, the layer of makeup felt thick and greasy on her sensitive skin. Her pores suffocated under a dusting of powder, and her mauve-colored eyelids felt weighted down.

When Mort had finished, he stepped back like an artist to judge his canvas and ordered, "Smile, Laurel."

"I'm afraid I'll crack my face."

"It's really quite an improvement. Notice how the eyes look so much larger. The lips are more full, almost pouting."

"The lips are pouting," she informed him. "Because the lips think they belong to a clown in a circus. The whole face, in fact, feels a bit silly."

"I'm sorry, dearie, if you don't like it. But you absolutely have to wear makeup for photos and television. The lights tend to wash out your features. Without shadow and highlight, you'll look like a colorless blob."

The door to the beauty parlor swung open, and Dane strode in. As soon as he caught sight of Laurel in the mirror, his dark eyes winked a greeting. Then he did a slow double take.

She held her breath, waiting for his response.

"Quite a change," he said slowly. He swiveled the barber chair so she faced him and rested one hand on each arm. For a long moment he gazed down at her. "Wash it off."

"Thank you," she said, breathing a heavy sigh of relief. If Cleo hadn't followed him into the room, she would have thrown her arms around Dane's neck and kissed him for all she was worth. Thank goodness he agreed with her assessment of this strange painted face.

While Mort voiced his objections, Laurel darted to the sink behind a red plastic curtain at the rear of the room. She scrubbed her face, listening to the argument raging behind her. She was shocked to hear Cleo say, "Dane is perfectly right. I agree that she looked more like a model, far more attractive. But that's not what we're after."

"If you want her to look plain," Mort answered peevishly, "I won't do anything at all. She's already been difficult about hair styling. Almost attacked me with a can of hairspray."

Dane's laughter bounced off the white walls of the beauty parlor. The sound filled Laurel with warm pleasure and silenced his associates. "Please excuse me," he apologized for his outburst. "I didn't get much sleep last night."

Laurel buried her cleansed face in a towel to stifle her own amusement. When she'd regained her composure, she returned to the room and said, "Mort is not exaggerating. I refuse to have my hair cut except to trim the ends. And I will not go out in public to promote natural products when I'm obviously wearing a ton of makeup."

Dane's voice was convincingly stern as he said, "Why don't you two step outside for a moment, and I'll try to talk some sense into her."

Once alone, their vague pretense at a cool business relationship vanished. As did the distance between them. Laurel turned her head against his chest and saw their embrace reflected in the mirror. "Don't they make a handsome couple?" she said.

"He looks a little tired," Dane commented. "But I think a kiss would wake him up."

"She's willing."

When their lips met, a now familiar sweetness flowed gently through Laurel's body. The beloved newness of his kiss had been worn smooth through repetition, as a piece of driftwood is beautifully sculpted by the waves.

They stood together for a moment, pleased with the marvelous progression of their affair. Laurel stayed within the circle of his arms but leaned back to see his face. "I wasn't being deliberately uncooperative."

"I know." He dropped a light kiss on her forehead. "Mort just didn't understand. I think Cleo does. Do you mind working with her?"

"I think I can handle it. Are you going to be here during this supposed make over?"

"I'd planned to be. Your appearance is all important to this project. Besides, I can't concentrate on anything else today, anyway. Everything I read, hear and touch reminds me of you." His eyes seemed to darken as he said, "Do you know what I'd rather be doing this morning?"

"I have a pretty fair idea."

"But we only have less than three hours until our one o'clock lunch date with the people who manufacture Meadow Flowers products. They want to meet you."

The practical concerns of Dane's business seemed intrusive when all she really wanted was to repeat last night's lovemaking. She snuggled against him, gave him a tight squeeze and moved away, reluctantly trying to find the balance between their business and personal relationships. Resolutely she returned to her chair before the mirror and critically eyed her reflection.

"Mort said I had to wear makeup under the lights. Or else I'd look like a colorless blob."

"He's probably right."

Yesterday she would have been insulted by Mort's assessment, but today everything was bright with serendipity. She caught Dane's eye in the mirror and intoned in a voice of doom, "Beware the Colorless Blob That Devoured Atlanta."

He stared back at her, his face frozen in an expression of mock terror. "Watch as she stalks down Peach Tree Street seeking constant transfusion, sucking the color from Ford pick-ups and Cadillacs."

"Until she blots out the very sun."

"This faceless woman from the mysterious mountains of Colorado."

"A Hammer film," she said.

"Starring Bela Lugosi and Laurel Janeway."

"Also known as Plain Janeway."

She stuck out her chin in a monster face and bounded menacingly out of the chair, fingers splayed like talons. "Next to go are the advertising executives," she growled.

"Unbeknownst to the Colorless Blob," he retaliated, "mild-mannered Dane MacGregor has an alternate identity. When the moon is full, he becomes . . . WolfDane."

The two monsters circled playfully, taking swipes at each other and baring their fangs, until WolfDane clasped the Colorless Blob in his arms and kissed her with mock ferocity.

He was breathing harder as he gazed at her. "Ah-ha, you're cured. WolfDane has put roses into the cheeks of the Blob."

"But I might be fading again. I think I need another transfusion."

"Gladly given."

His kiss was gentle and lingering, and she knew he was as reluctant as she to return to the business of promoting Meadow Flowers. "Maybe tonight," she said, "we could work on a permanent cure."

"Count on it. How do you know about Hammer Films, anyway? You're much too young to have seen the original movies, and I thought you didn't watch television."

"I didn't watch television while I lived in the mountains," she corrected him. "When I first had my own apartment in Denver, many were the nights that I sat in front of the box with popcorn on my knee watching the late, late show."

"I've got a lot to learn about you," he said, disengaging himself and pointing her toward the mirrors. "But right now we have to work."

"Yessir." Laurel obediently took her place in the adjustable barber chair. "Why do I feel like I'm at the dentist's office?"

"Mort's brother-in-law is a dentist. That's where he got that great set of caps."

"Why did Mort leave New York?"

"Painful memories, I guess. He left after he was divorced. It wasn't a friendly separation. There was a big custody fight over two of the cutest kids I've ever seen."

"That must be why he's so bitter." Laurel's family life had always been warm and content, so that she was genuinely sympathetic toward those who hadn't been so lucky. "Poor Mort."

"Poor everybody who goes through divorce." He picked up a wide makeup brush and dusted off her nose. "Husbands and wives. Children and parents. It's all very sad, but life goes on."

"You seem to know what you're talking about. Personal experience?"

He made himself busy, rearranging the pots of makeup and pencils and brushes. He wouldn't meet her eyes. "You didn't look like yourself with all that stuff on your face."

"And you don't look like yourself right now."

"I don't want to talk about it. Not now. Let's just enjoy our moment of happiness."

"Maybe you ought to use that makeup to draw yourself a smile. You don't look happy." Laurel wondered what Dane was seeing when he stared into the mirror. Last night when he'd spoken about lies and disguises, she'd thought of endless funhouse reflections. While she watched him, another mask seemed to be forming. There was a hardness to his jaw. The light went out of his eyes. "Please tell me, Dane."

"It'll have to wait. We have other business to attend to."

"Please. You said before that you'd never been married. Was that true?"

"Sure was." He pivoted and faced her. She didn't recognize the tone in his voice. Bitter? Hurt? "I didn't need to be married. My mother walked down the aisle often enough for everybody in the family. Right now she's on her fourth husband."

"That must have been hard for you."

"Laurel, I promise we'll talk about this. But it's going to have to be at another time. Okay?"

He opened the door and called out for Mort and Cleo, effectively ending their conversation. The revelation of Dane's unsettled childhood gave Laurel something to chew on, but she filed it in the back of her mind. She needed all her wits about her to deal with the proposed make over.

"One inch," she said to Mort. "And one inch only."

"No perm?"

"Absolutely not."

"How about if I paint on more sun streaks?"

Cleo's first comment of the morning was in a far less acidic tone than Laurel remembered. "Don't bother, Mort. Her hair has already been professionally lightened, hasn't it, Laurel?"

"Not in a beauty shop. I do it myself with a rinse made of lemon, dried marigold flowers and white wine. Then I dry my hair in the sun."

The shocked expressions on their faces made her smile. "If you want some really bizarre information, wait until I tell you what I drink in my tea."

"Whatever it is must be working," Mort said. "Cleo tells me you're twenty-six and used to work as an executive secretary, too. I would have thought from the texture of your skin that you were barely out of your teens."

Laurel glanced at Cleo, who studiously avoided meeting her eyes. Apparently her chat with Dane had included a résumé of Laurel's age and work history. What other information had he passed along? It might not be wise, Laurel reflected, to give Cleo too much ammunition.

"Well?" Mort asked. "What's your secret?"

"For one thing," Laurel said, "I don't use foundation makeup unless I absolutely have to."

"You'll have to for photographs and television."

"I know," she said, finding Dane's reflection in the mirror and grinning. "Or else I'll be a colorless blob."

Dane turned away—probably to keep from laughing, Laurel thought. He sauntered to a bright yellow director's chair and settled into it. Apparently he intended to leave this process up to Laurel. In a brisk tone she said, "Why don't you give me some idea of what you'd like to do,

Mort? Then I'll tell you what's acceptable from my view-point."

They negotiated the styling of her hair, and Laurel agreed to the addition of light highlights around her face, but no perm and no more cutting than an inch.

She allowed Mort to pluck her eyebrows to a more flat-tering shape and to dye them a slightly darker brown. Likewise, he convinced her to dye her thick blond eye-lashes. The dark sable fringe around her eyes made a dra-matic difference.

Laurel blinked at her reflection in the mirror. "This is wonderful, Mort. I love it. It's permanent, isn't it?"

"About once a month you'll need a touch up, but it won't wash off." Mort regarded her critically. "Which is prob-ably wise. You're the type to go diving in swimming pools and ruining your mascara."

As a woman she wanted to ask Dane's opinion, but she was beginning to catch a glimmer of understanding as to what it meant to be a model. Laurel decided to wait until Mort's packaging was complete. Besides, she could see warm approval in Dane's gaze. Though he hadn't said one word, his smile and an occasional raising of eyebrows communicated his appreciation for her new image.

Belinda was more vocal. She tapped on the door and entered Mort's workshop. "Laurel, you've got twenty minutes before you need to leave for that lunch date." She paused, head cocked to one side, and nodded before con-tinuing. "And you look ready. Honey, your hair and eyes are terrific."

"All she needs," Mort said, "is the dress."

Laurel remembered Dane's urban-cowboy outfit and Mort's first attempt at makeup. With suspicion in her voice she asked, "What dress?"

"It's my own design," he said, dragging her from the chair. "The Meadow Flowers dress."

"What if it doesn't fit?" she asked hopefully. "Can't I just wear what I have on?"

"It'll fit."

He led her past the photo studio into a large dressing room with racks of clothes and two full-length mirrors. Feather boas and swatches of sequined material draped across perfectly proportioned mannequins. A large bouquet of wildflowers reflected double in another mirror on a makeup table.

"When I started this design," Mort said, "I was thinking about wood sprites. I wanted something natural, but provocative. A sort of Mother Nature motif with a bared shoulder."

"Listen, Mort. I am not going to lunch in a fig leaf no matter how fashionable."

"That's what Dane said. He told me to save the shoulder for the photo layouts, design something simple for now, so you could appear in public without looking outlandish. Respectable was the word he used. To create an honest, believable image for the product, we couldn't have you looking like a reject from the Isadora Duncan school."

The dress he pulled from the rack was charming. The basic design featured a full-cut shirtwaist dress of apricot silk. Stitching around the cuffs and collar was a gentle, creamy white, a color echoed in the fancifully embroidered flowers that twined down the front placket and around the wide belt. A soft cardigan jacket with slightly padded shoulders and three-quarter-length sleeves completed the feminine yet businesslike outfit.

"This is lovely!" Laurel exclaimed.

"This color is for autumn," he said with a smug smile. "I've repeated the theme in turquoise and black, and in a minty spring green. But I thought you should wear the apricot tone first to take advantage of your tan."

"You talk as if I'm going to be wearing these outfits for years."

"If the campaign is a success, you will be. Well, hurry and get dressed, Laurel."

"I'll be glad to, as soon as you leave."

"Come, come, child. Let's not be modest. It's my creation, after all. I should be the first to see it."

"But it's my body that will be wearing it. Now we both know how stubborn I can be, and I don't intend to undress while you're standing here."

"I'll be waiting in the photo studio next door," he said with a resigned sigh. "The shoes, purse, slip and panty hose are in that box."

The beige slip and silky panty hose were precisely her size, and Laurel wondered briefly how that bit of magic had been accomplished. Probably someone like Mort who was involved in designing women's clothing could decipher dress sizes as easily as she could identify plants.

She slipped the dress over her head, reveling in the luxurious smoothness of pure silk. Belted and buttoned, it fit perfectly. The length was just right, and the light fabric molded the swell of her hips. A full-cut bodice allowed for easy movement. She swirled the skirt in front of the mirror, and her long hair followed in a graceful swish.

Even the shoes, ivory pumps with two-inch heels, were comfortable. She transferred her wallet, sunglasses and a packet of tissue to the matching clutch purse and glanced once more in the mirror. She'd never looked better. Without a doubt Dane would be impressed.

Laurel swept into the photo studio where the whole Meadow Flowers creative and production team was gathered. Mort, Cleo, Fred and Belinda exclaimed with appropriate oohs and aahs, but she waited for Dane's reaction.

He was sprawled in a director's chair, his long legs stretched before him. His chin rested wearily on one fist, and his eyelids drooped lazily. He looked tired, she thought, and as grumpy as a male lion waiting for his dinner.

When she spun in a circle, he roused himself from his half-asleep pose and went to her. She stood very still, looking up at him, her heart beating quickly in anticipation.

"You're beautiful," he said softly.

"Thank you, Dane."

He took her arm and turned triumphantly to his staff. "I was right, wasn't I? She looks fantastic. Even better than I thought she would."

"I'd buy anything she's selling," Mort enthused. "Too bad we can't market the dress along with the product."

Freddy silently clicked candid shots, pausing only an instant to make an "okay" sign with thumb and forefinger.

Belinda's wide smile of approval managed to encompass both Laurel and Dane as a couple.

Even Cleo had a compliment. "I think we've got a winner, boys and girls. I know the Ultra Taste people will be pleased."

"Ultra Taste?" Laurel questioned. "What do they have to do with Meadow Flowers?"

"They're the manufacturers," Cleo explained. "Meadow Flowers will be one of their subsidiaries."

"Ultra Taste," Laurel repeated disbelievingly. She felt Dane's hand tighten on her arm. "No one mentioned anything about them."

"Does it make a difference?" Cleo asked with sly unconcern.

"Of course it does. Ultra Taste is responsible for several brands of sugar-coated children's cereals. And the most artificially flavored of granola bars. And candy. They also package a nondecaffeinated coffee, don't they?"

"And cookies and beauty products," Cleo added. "Ultra Taste is one of the biggest and most diverse manufacturers."

"What can those people possibly know about natural products?" Laurel asked. "They've been systematically poisoning the consumer for years."

"They're really not so bad," Cleo put in. Her contrite expression was obviously staged for Dane's benefit, as though this revelation about Ultra Taste had been nothing more than an unintentional slip. Laurel knew better. Cleo had deliberately saved this piece of information for the most devastating moment. Laurel wrenched her arm free from Dane's grasp and glared at him. "Why didn't you tell me?"

The pained expression on his face was enough explanation for her. She was certain his omission had been deliberate.

Though it was her own fault that she hadn't clarified Meadow Flowers' affiliations, Laurel felt as if she'd been used. Here she was in Atlanta, preening in her new finery and thoughtlessly getting ready to represent a company whose products she couldn't endorse.

Laurel couldn't decide which was more infuriating, Dane's deception or her own blind trust. She ignored Cleo's falsely conciliatory palaver about the exemplary labor practices of the giant conglomerate: day-care centers for employees, outstanding retirement benefits, equal pay for work of equal value.

"Mister MacGregor," Laurel said through clenched teeth, "may I speak to you alone, please?"

With a sick grin for the rest of his staff, he followed her back into the dressing room and closed the door. "I'm sorry, Laurel."

"How could you? I forgave your first deception about Meadow Flowers because I thought you didn't have time to explain. But this is appalling. I can't possibly represent Ultra Taste as an herbal manufacturer. The thought is absurd."

"I meant to explain. But every time I got started other things interfered."

"You never had any intention of manufacturing my products, either. That was all a lie."

"Not really. The nutritionists from Ultra Taste are sincerely interested in your input. They want Meadow Flowers to be the best products they can be."

"'Sincere'? You really expect me to believe that the people who stock grocery shelves with Sugar Shock cereal are sincere?"

She paced across the room, the chic loveliness of her ensemble mocking her from the mirrors. She'd been packaged, she thought, wrapped and designed to trick the public into buying yet another useless lotion with the implied promise that they would look like the new Laurel Janeway. If they didn't read the list of ingredients, they would be impressed.

And what about Dane? She turned to face him. Her own gullibility enraged her. How easily she had been deceived by his broad shoulders and dark eyes. For he, too, was packaged. She thought of all the identities he'd displayed for her: flyboy pilot, urban cowboy, executive, lover.

He had costumes and manners for each package, and she'd bought the overall effect without reading the labels, without discerning what was inside. His surface persona was virile, caring and warm. Underneath, his heart was cold. Those full lips were capable of lying. Even the hurt she saw in his eyes was probably an artificial response to her disdain. How could he feel hurt? Nothing was genuine or true in his world of image.

A flicker of her own pain kindled deep within her. What about last night? Had that been part of his game plan? An angry flush colored her cheeks as she considered that terrible possibility. He must have figured he could seduce her into ignoring her ethical objections, if she ever found out about Ultra Taste.

"Is there a telephone in this room?" she snapped. "I want to talk to my attorney."

"May I explain something first?"

"I don't owe you the time for an explanation. My contract has an escape clause. Perhaps I could escape while I still have a shred of dignity intact."

"Laurel, please."

"Please what?"

"Be reasonable."

"I am," she said. "I am using my rational reasonable brain to work out all these connections, but this is an impossible problem. There can be no logic with all these false premises. Have you been honest with me about anything?"

"You know I have."

"I know nothing."

"Why are you carrying on like this? At least give these nutritionists a chance to state their case."

"No. Absolutely not. I will not listen to any more lies. Please excuse me, Dane. I'll be dressed and gone in a minute, and then you're free to con some other dumb model into fronting for Ultra Taste."

"Is that really what you think?" He crossed the room in two wide strides and grabbed her arms, forcing her to confront him. "Do you think you can be replaced with a snap of my fingers? Forget Ultra Taste and Meadow Flowers—look at me. Didn't last night mean anything to you?"

"A better-than-average one-night stand." She tried to speak with conviction, but the words caught in her throat. Her emotions were in such a tangle that she choked on her words.

"You don't lie well, Laurel."

"Thanks for the expert opinion."

His grip hardened, and she saw a flash in his eyes. Anger? How dare he be angry? He was the one who'd wronged her.

"I haven't lied to you."

"It doesn't matter what you call it, Dane. Conveniently forgetting to tell me something still counts as deception. I don't know what else I expected. Misleading people is your profession. You're probably so used to stretching the truth that you don't even know what it is."

"I know what I feel for you, Laurel. And if this feeling isn't good and pure and honest, then you're right. I don't know the truth anymore. Last night was special for me. You made me happier than I ever thought was possible. And I think it was the same for you."

She refused to look into his eyes. His words were so convincing. His voice sounded so sincere. She could feel herself being reeled in like a rainbow trout on a hook. No matter how hard she thrashed and protested, the tensile strength of the night they'd shared would be stronger.

He released his grasp and turned away from her. Hands in his pockets, he started to talk. "I know I'm not the sort of man you approve of. I didn't get to where I am in this business by being a nice guy all the time. There were some hard decisions to make along the way. And I haven't always been in the right. I've stretched the truth. It doesn't make me feel good to admit that, but I will. And I'm proud of what I've accomplished."

She could see his profile in the makeup mirror. An image of his image. What should she believe? Her aching heart yearned to accept him, no matter what he was or what he had been. Yet her conscience held her back. If there was no foundation of trust between them, nothing else could exist.

He continued. "The first time I saw you, I wanted you for this advertising campaign. You weren't a living breathing woman to me. Just a model. Somebody whose picture would look good on a package. But that changed. I still wanted you. God, how I wanted you. But I didn't give a damn about Meadow Flowers or MacGregor and Associates or Ultra Taste."

His deep voice was soft and caressing as he said simply, "I'm falling in love with you."

She wrapped her fingers around the back of a wooden chair and held on for dear life. He hadn't mentioned love last night. They'd spoken of passion and desire, consummated the physical attraction that had tormented both of them, but there had been no declarations of commitment. Why did he have to choose this moment to tell her? Now she couldn't believe him.

Though she wanted to accept his love, she could no longer trust him. The right thing to do was to throw his words back in his face and run as fast and as far as she could.

"I'm not just saying that to change your mind," he assured her.

"It's an awfully convenient time for you to come to that decision. Please, Dane, don't lie to me about love."

"I wouldn't. It's a word I don't take lightly, and a feeling that I haven't given often. Probably not often enough. Feeling love scares me, Laurel. Scares me almost as much as the thought of you leaving."

"Why didn't you consider that before? Why didn't you tell me about Ultra Taste?"

"Because I suspected what your reaction would be. I thought with more time you wouldn't reject the whole project."

"You expected me to change? After I was dressed in silk with liner on my eyes, I was supposed to forget any sort of ethics I might have had, is that it?"

"When you phrase it that way, it sounds ridiculous."

"Because it is. It doesn't matter what I'm wearing, Dane. I'm always going to be the same person inside."

"I know that now. And I know I should have talked this over with you. Believe me, Laurel. I'm not trying to trick you into representing a product you don't truly believe in."

He paused, seeming to search for exactly the right words. If this was an act, Laurel thought, it was a darn good one.

"It wasn't right," he said, "for me to talk about love. This isn't the right time. I wasn't consciously trying to manipulate you, but my instincts were dead wrong. Damn, I always seem to be apologizing to you."

"I'm sorry too, Dane. Sorry that you don't trust me enough to be honest with me."

"What's ridiculous is that I had the same initial objections to Ultra Taste that you have. Believe me, Laurel, I checked them out thoroughly before I started bidding on the Meadow Flowers contract. Cleo's spiel about labor practices is true. They're a company in transition. If I can convince you of that, will you forgive me? Can we go back to the way we were?"

"I don't put any conditions on love."

"But part of caring for someone is being able to trust them, and I've lost your trust. I want you to give me one last chance."

"A chance for what?"

"To prove that bringing you to Atlanta wasn't a con job. I won't appeal to your feelings for me—whatever they might be—but I will call on your sense of fair play."

"What do you want me to do?"

"Meet with the people from Ultra Taste. I'm not asking you to disregard your prejudices about the products they manufacture. Be as tough as you want. But once you've spoken to these nutritionists, I think you'll understand why I didn't make a point of telling you that Meadow Flowers is their subsidiary."

She sighed deeply and considered his argument. In her opinion it was doubtful that she could find any reaonable justification for the recipes used by Ultra Taste. They set the standard for high sugar content. Yet his point was well taken. She was acting out of preconceived prejudice. It was only fair to allow these touted nutritionists to state their case.

"All right, Dane. I'll go to the luncheon, but I warn you that I'm going to be critical."

"I have one more request. Give me tonight, Laurel. One night to make everything clear between us."

"No."

He winced visibly, but she continued with resolve. "I want tonight for myself, Dane. I need the space to think, to make sense of what I'm feeling. And I can't do that when I'm with you."

"Really? Do I affect you like that?"

"You do."

He turned to her, a devastatingly handsome smile bringing his deep dimples to life. "Then there's hope for me."

9

DANE MACGREGOR had run fresh out of miracle cures. His ability to solve supposedly insurmountable problems wasn't working with Laurel. As they left the restaurant after lunch and strolled to the nearby parking lot, where his silver-gray BMW was parked, he reviewed his strategies. He'd sent flowers. He'd made a special trip to bring her back to Atlanta. He'd taken her to dinner. Their lovemaking had been superlative.

His mind skimmed over the perfect details of their mating. She was beautifully responsive. Her supple flesh tantalized him even now, and the memory of her inventiveness inspired a renewed arousal in him.

He gazed down at her flowing blond hair as she matched him stride for stride. Her blue eyes were focused straight ahead, and her jaw was so tightly clenched that he doubted she could have talked to him even if she'd wanted to. What had gone wrong? By all rights she should be clinging to his arm.

Somehow the scripts for this scenario had been interchanged. Though he'd done everything he could to play the part of the charming attentive lover, she was treating him with the sort of disdain reserved for six-eyed, twelve-legged creatures from outer space. WolfDane, he thought ruefully. Maybe that was the problem. He'd been too kind. Maybe it would be more effective to drag her screaming into the sunset.

"I thought the luncheon went well," he said, opening the car door for her and watching as she swivelled her silken legs inside. "Extremely well."

"Yes, it did." She fastened her seat belt, slipped on an oversized pair of sunglasses and stared intently through the windshield at the Walk-Don't Walk sign on the street corner. "Are we going back to your office?"

"No, it's after three o'clock. That should be enough for one day."

"Then I would appreciate a lift to my motel."

Dane circled the car, considering alternatives. He didn't want to take her back to her motel. Not unless he was invited to stay, and her tone, on top of her earlier words, made it clear that she expected to spend the rest of the day and night alone. As he slid behind the wheel, he decided to point out that she owed him an apology.

"I thought you'd be impressed with the Meadow Flowers nutritionists," he ventured cautiously. "I was sure that once you met them it wouldn't matter who they were associated with."

"Their competence is not the issue, Dane."

"Of course it is." He started the engine and turned the air conditioner on full. "You were in complete accord with their philosophy—working within the system for change—weren't you?"

"I understand their motivation. And I wasn't aware of the many outstanding labor practices of Ultra Taste. I'm encouraged by the fact that if Meadow Flowers is successful, Ultra Taste will move toward more wholesome ingredients in all their products. Also, I didn't miss the reason that they selected MacGregor and Associates to promote Meadow Flowers."

"My reputation for honesty," he said with a satisfied grin. "Turning in the most comprehensive package for the lowest bid didn't hurt."

His disarming smile was not returned. She was as distant as an oil painting in a museum. He tried another tack.

"You made a good impression, Laurel. You were beautiful, poised and wise, and I thank you for that. Mac-Gregor and Associates was selected for the Meadow Flowers campaign precisely because they wanted a new fresh look. And you gave them what they wanted."

"Isn't that terrific." Her sunglasses made it impossible for him to read the expression in her blue eyes as she quickly glanced toward him and turned her gaze back out the window. "Your agency is terrific. Despite my misgivings, the Meadow Flowers program sounds very terrific. Most of all, you are terrific. Now would you please take me home."

"I don't get it. Why are you staring out the window like a great stone face? You haven't been deceived. You've been recruited. You've been appointed general of the great natural-food crusade."

"Look, I'm willing to admit that you were absolutely on target about the Meadow Flowers nutritionists. But that's not the point. And you know it."

Her deep sigh cut through him. He knew she was disappointed in him, and her reproach pained him more than her anger. Dane was unaccustomed to falling short of anybody's expectations.

The one constant in his life was success. His achievements could fill a record book. From kindergarten through graduate school, he had been voted Most Likely to Succeed. The star quarterback. The straight-A student. The fastest driver. The president of JayCees. The boss.

Sure, there had been a few missteps along the way, but his accomplishments were substantial enough to be gratifying. Instead, his success tasted bitter because it wasn't enough for Laurel. He had to try something else, something she would find irresistible.

"What do you want from me?" he demanded as he guided the car into traffic. "I'm well-off, passably good-looking and generally well thought of in the community. What more do you want?"

"I can't find fault with your image. But it's just that. An image. You're so busy manipulating people and things that I don't know you. Who is Dane MacGregor? What makes him tick? Why can't he level with me?"

"I'm trying. Give me the benefit of the doubt. I just forgot to tell you that Ultra Taste was involved."

"Like you forgot to mention that your wildflower bouquet was just lying around the office. And you forgot to tell me you were coming to Colorado to bid on my generator. Please give me credit for being more astute than that."

While they rode in silence, Dane concocted a plan. He wasn't going to take her back to the motel. The thought of watching her door slam in his face made him miserable. Somewhere else, he thought. They had to go somewhere else. He turned onto the highway heading east.

"Since you approved of the Meadow Flowers program," he said, "may I assume that you intend to stay here in Atlanta and act as their representative?"

"That's right. I plan to fulfill my contract with you. Now that I understand the goals of those nutritionists and have been reassured about their ability to create a natural product, I feel positive about working for Meadow Flowers. From a purely business standpoint, everything is fine."

"Meaning what?"

"This is not the way to my motel. Where are you taking me?"

"I thought I might feed you to an alligator in the Oke-fenokee Swamp."

"We're nowhere near there, are we?"

"Same state."

"Listen, Dane. I'm not in the mood for sightseeing. Please take me back to my motel."

"Why? So you can brood and pout and drink valium tea?"

"Valerian," she corrected. "Valerian-root tea."

"Whatever."

He drove inexorably onward. The view of Stone Mountain with its giant sculpture of Confederate heroes rose before them, clearly marking one possible destination. Dane watched the exit signs. There was one last bit of business he needed to carry out while they were on this route. Since she'd agreed to stay in Atlanta, this detail was imperative.

"In any case," she said with a firm hard edge to her voice, "if I choose to drink tea and pout, that is my decision. I want some space to sit and think and sort things out in my head. The least you can do is respect my wishes."

"We'll get to your motel," he assured her. "Just sit back and enjoy the ride. I'll get you home. Eventually."

"I don't appreciate these tactics, Dane. This kind of thing went out with Tarzan and Jane."

"I can't help myself. Something about you brings out the caveman in me."

"The Neanderthal," she confirmed.

"Neanderthal Man and the Colorless Blob," he teased, thrusting out his jaw in imitation of a primordial beast and making vaguely obscene grunting noises.

"Damn it, Dane. You stop this car."

"I can't. I'm in the fast lane. Besides, this is just suburbs. There's nothing exciting here."

"You want excitement? All right. If you don't pull off at the very next exit, I am going to explode."

He merged across the highway lanes and made the exit, cruising past a small grocery store and down a quiet suburban street. Turning off the ignition, he faced her and said lightly, "Something on your mind?"

"I've had enough. Enough of your games and your convenient forgetting and your clever manipulations."

Her voice was low and controlled, a tone more frightening to him than outright screaming. Frightening? Was he scared? He was experiencing the same sharpening of the senses and accelerated punch of adrenaline that he had when she'd walked out of the meeting yesterday.

She kept doing this to him. Against his will. He didn't remember giving her that prerogative, but somehow she'd taken control of his mental well-being.

"You want to talk?" he challenged. "Let's talk about manipulation. Let's discuss the way you keep bouncing in and out of my life. How about your seductive little soak in the bathtub in the mountains? Or don't you want to remember that ploy? It seems that you don't object to the games, as long as you're making up the rules."

"You're right," she admitted quietly. "And I'm sorry. That was cutesy and stupid, and I'm sorry I did it. Also, I'm not proud of walking out on you yesterday."

She removed her sunglasses and subjected him to a direct clear gaze, a look that allowed him no hiding place. It seemed that she could see through to his soul. No secrets. No escapes.

"After last night," she said, "I thought the games were over. I trusted you completely, gave you a part of myself more precious than the physical giving. I loved you, Dane."

"Past tense?" He was bewildered and angry.

"I don't know. Maybe we've gone too fast. Maybe we don't know each other well enough to share ourselves. I'm only sure of the hurt. For some reason you didn't trust me enough to tell me about the Ultra Taste connection. And that hurts."

"I didn't want to make you angry." He wanted to hold her, to kiss away the hurt. "I didn't want to take the chance that you might walk out again."

"Let's clarify this right now. I will never again leave you over a business dispute. It's just packaging, wrapping paper and ribbons, not important as long as the contents are above reproach. You, Dane MacGregor, are what's important to me. Our relationship is the surprise inside the package."

"How can I make it right?"

"No more tricks," she said. "No more driving off in the car when I tell you I don't want to go. Tell me everything, every detail. Respect me enough to let me make my own decisions. When you want an answer from me, just ask the question."

He wanted to ask if she loved him, if she would love him forever. But he feared her response. He hadn't intended for all this to happen. Holding back the information about Ultra Taste hadn't been a conscious decision to con her into doing something she didn't want to do. Likewise, this teasing abduction had seemed the most natural way to get her attention, to convince her. That was how he operated. Was he really so out of touch with honest reactions that he couldn't perceive them in Laurel?

"I'd like to ask a direct question," he said. "Will you stay in Atlanta?"

"I already said I would."

"How long?"

"I want to pursue the Meadow Flowers campaign. But that's not the main reason. I'll stay as long as it takes to make a decision about our relationship."

"What kind of decision?"

"Whether or not a long-term commitment is possible." She reached across the car to rest her slender hand on his thigh. "I don't want to spend all our time together fighting. You know, the very first time I saw you, before you had spoken or moved, I felt apprehension and excitement. Here was this man who'd fallen from the clouds. I didn't know what to think."

He rested his hand on hers, encouraging her and hoping she would repeat the words he wanted to hear.

"My life had been simple, calm and contented," she continued. "I wasn't planning any changes. But they happened. You made them happen. I'm still trying to sift all my reactions. I know it's going to take time, but I want to give us a chance. We have something special; it won't be denied or refused. You are the reason I'm staying in Atlanta, Dane. We need time to learn about each other. Time to find out who we are. Apart and together."

"Another question: may I kiss you?"

Her refusal was gentle. "It's a question of timing."

"I think we should seal our pact to learn more about each other... with a kiss."

"Have you been listening to me, Dane? We have to be more than just physical together."

"But let's not ignore the physical part. Really, a kiss is the best way to confirm our sincerity, don't you think? We're a long way beyond handshakes."

Her grin was spontaneous, and Dane felt himself relax. Something he had said had been right. She wasn't ready to acquiesce, but the grin showed a certain willingness to cooperate. He was reminded of when they had first met and she had deigned to show him to her cabin.

"Maybe," she said with a hint of mischief in her voice, "maybe we should make a blood vow."

"And what sort of heathen practice is that?"

"We used to do it in the mountains to seal undying promises and swear each other to secrecy. First you each nick your thumb with a pocketknife. Then you rub your thumbs together, mingling the blood. It's virtually impossible to betray a blood brother or sister."

"What a shame! I left my pocketknife at home."

"Then maybe you're right. I guess I'll have to settle for that kiss."

His hand caressed her satin cheek. He held her for a moment with his gaze, admiring the bright sparkle in her blue eyes. He didn't comprehend the need for further study of their relationship. His feelings were crystal clear to him. Slowly he lowered his mouth to hers.

The softness of her lips thrilled him, giving him the inexplicable joy he always felt when they touched. Her body arched toward him, but they joined only at the lips.

"Laurel," he breathed, "unfasten your seat belt."

"What?"

"Unfasten your seat belt and come over here."

"I don't think that would be a good idea."

"I'm too old for this," he said, tacitly agreeing, slumping back behind the wheel. "I don't know how you get me into these weird situations. I'm a respected businessman. I shouldn't be making out in the middle of an afternoon on a street corner. Can we go back to your motel?"

"Nope. I still want to spend the rest of the day by myself."

"I hope this getting-to-know-each-other period of yours doesn't include celibacy. Because that wouldn't be honest or fair."

"You're right, Dane. And it doesn't." She grinned again. "I think it's too late for me to play virgin."

"Then why can't we spend the night together?"

"Let me try to explain. I lived alone for a long time. Really alone. Without a telephone or a television set or even a radio. Coming into a city again is enough to throw me for a loop, much less trying to untangle everything I'm feeling about you. I need these hours by myself. All these things are coming at me so fast. I need to think."

She wasn't sure if that made good sense, but it was the truth. Her inclination was to forget logic and simply enjoy the tingling sensations he aroused in her, to give herself over to pure pleasure. Yet their relationship was too important for that. There had to be an understanding before they went any farther along this winding path. She needed to be grounded, to study the unfamiliar landmarks.

"All right, Laurel. Even though I'd rather throw you over my shoulder like the insensitive Neanderthal that I am, I'll respect your wishes." He shook his head and stared through the windshield. "Well, well, look at this."

"What?"

"We have an audience." He pointed to a small boy, probably four or five years old, who had taken up a position directly in front of the car.

"I think I'd better investigate," Dane said. "He might be the vice squad in a clever undercover disguise."

Laurel climbed out of the car to watch as Dane squatted down to the child's height. "Do you like this car?" he asked.

"It's real pretty," the boy drawled. "My name is Douglas, and I'm five. Can I wash your car for you, Mister?" Douglas scratched his ear and considered before making the final pitch. "Fifty cents?"

"That's a pretty good deal." Dane smiled. "Listen, Douglas, has your mother ever told you about speaking to strangers?"

"Yessir." He jumped back a few paces. "Mama says I ain't supposed to. Never."

"I'm not going to hurt you," Dane said. "But your Mama is right. Do you know where Mr. Bell lives?"

"Yessir." He pointed to a split-level house with dark gray siding and white trim. "He's my neighbor. You know Mr. Bell?"

"I sure do."

"Then you ain't no stranger. Can I wash your car?"

Dane kept a straight face and explained, "I'm still a stranger until Mr. Bell shows you that he and I know each other. I'm going up to the door to see if he's home, and if he waves to you, it's okay."

"What about her?" Douglas said, pointing to Laurel.

"Same goes for her."

Dane stood up and came around to the passenger window. "Do you mind? This should only take a few minutes. I have some business to talk over with Lawrence Bell."

"I don't mind at all."

As she watched him heading up the neat sidewalk, she couldn't help smiling. She never would have thought Dane would be so good with children. That made sense, though. He got along with everyone. What was odd was that they had ended up in his friend's neighborhood. She got out of the car and stretched.

Mr. Bell was in. As soon as Dane waved, Douglas went into action, dashing up to his own house and dragging a garden hose across the neat green lawn.

"This car sure is pretty," he said. "I'm going to get one just like it." He raced back to the house and turned on the faucet. With both hands he aimed the nozzle at the hood and sprayed. "Are you married?" he asked Laurel.

"Nope." She moved well out of the range of Douglas's enthusiastic car wash. Mort would be furious if she ruined her silk Meadow Flowers dress. "Nope, I'm not married. Are you?"

"Sarah Beth keeps asking me, but I ain't." Douglas sprayed the hubcaps. "How come you were kissing if you aren't married?"

"You don't have to be married to kiss. Kissing just means that you like somebody."

"Sarah Beth wants me to kiss her, but I told her we had to wait until we're married."

"That's probably a smart move, Douglas."

Dane's business, as promised, only took a moment. He bounded down the sidewalk to join them.

"Nice work, Douglas." He glanced over at Laurel. "And what were you two talking about?"

Douglas answered for her. "Marriage."

"Oh, no, you don't," Dane informed his pint-sized competitor. "This lady is taken."

WHEN DANE DROPPED her off, Laurel gave his hand a squeeze and hurried into her motel room. More discussion wasn't necessary. Inside her room she leaned against the cool metal door, took a deep breath and closed her eyes. So much had happened in the course of twenty-four hours.

During the year she'd lived in the Colorado mountains, there had never been a day so full of talk and changes as this one. Her solitary life had been blissfully silent. A big event had been to see whether three or five hummingbirds had come to the feeder.

Atlanta would take some getting used to, she decided, kicking off her pumps and striding toward the bedroom in a swirl of apricot silk.

Her new clothes, new city and new job were spread before her. Her life was as full of promise as a blank canvas, primed for an artist's strokes. And a wonderful picture had already been sketched out—her brand-new relationship with Dane.

He had already said he loved her. Though she doubted that his definition of love matched hers, his declaration was a good positive start. Given enough time, surely he would come to see the importance of sharing, trust and companionship. Love everlasting took careful nurturing in order to continually replenish itself.

She was confident that he would come around to her way of thinking. Strange, he'd brought her here for the express purpose of changing her appearance and molding her into a model—something she most definitely was not. Yet she was demanding changes from him, insisting that he forego his usual machinations and glib facade. Intimate sharing in the deepest sense was obviously difficult for him.

Carefully Laurel hung her Meadow Flowers dress in the closet. The emperor's—or empress's—new clothes were lovely. But underneath she would always be Plain Janeway, the colorless blob from Colorado.

She put on wide-legged walking shorts and strolled the area around the motel until she found a small supermarket. While she bought essential groceries Laurel reflected on the contribution that Meadow Flowers could make. Unless a shopper went to a specialized health-food store, the selection of teas and cereals was dismal in the average groceteria, one like this. Nutritious dairy products like unflavored yogurt weren't available, either, and only one brand of whole-grain bread was offered here. The various departments should provide a choice. If natural herbal products proved to be successful, the marketplace could be changed.

On the way back to her motel, she walked briskly with her two bags. Her body must be getting used to the humidity: she felt as vibrant as the crimson sunset that cast long shadows from the tall buildings. The grass and trees were so lush and green. Atlanta wasn't the terrible place she'd first imagined. All those oak trees would be beautiful in autumn.

Back in her motel room, the telephone was ringing. She deposited her groceries and ran to pick it up. "Hello . . . ?"

"Where were you?" Dane demanded.

"Out foraging for supplies." Even though she could hear his irritation crackling over the telephone wires, the sound of his voice gave her an almost physical pleasure.

"I was worried, Laurel. I don't want you out running around after dark."

"It's not dark. There's the most spectacular sunset. And the temperature must have dropped ten degrees."

"Should I bring over some dinner? If you don't want to see me, I can leave it outside the door and knock twice."

"Are you near a window?"

"Why? Are you going to suggest that I jump out?"

"Look out your window at the sunset and take three deep breaths." She waited, taking her own deep breaths before asking, "Doesn't that feel better?"

"Slightly," he admitted. "I'd love to be up in that sky in an ultralight. You can't imagine what it's like to be in the middle of pink cloud, looking down at tiny buildings and lights."

"It must be wonderful to be part of the sunset."

"Want to try it?"

"Not that wonderful," she quickly demurred. "Maybe someday, but don't go chartering any planes."

"I know of a flight we can take together. Without leaving the ground. I can be there in half an hour for takeoff."

"Let's make reservations for tomorrow. I really need to spend some time by myself."

"Until tomorrow. Will you have dinner with me at my house?"

"I'd like that very much. I'm curious to see where you live."

"I wish there was something we could do tonight," he persisted. The tone of his voice left no question about his preferred activity, yet surprisingly he proceeded with an innocent question. "What's your favorite color?"

"Probably blue. Why?"

"I'm just trying to get to know you. What about your favorite kind of music?"

"I like classical, and I have a real fondness for Windham Hill records—William Ackerman and George Winston."

"Finally," he said. "We have something in common. Your favorite kind of pet?"

"I'm a dog person."

"Me, too. That's your second correct answer. One more and you win the prize."

"Which is?"

"I come over to your motel and take you out to dinner?"

"Tomorrow," she said.

Laurel gently replaced the receiver, and silence filled the room. The peace and quiet was luxurious, a restorative after the long, event-filled day at MacGregor and Associates. She closed her eyes and remembered: Mort with his overeager clippers, the warm friendliness of Belinda, Cleo's acid tongue, Freddy clicking pictures. And Dane.

He'd shown her a whole series of identities, but she worried most about the little boy whose mother had been married four times. Had he been abandoned? Had he been unloved? It was no wonder, she thought, that he felt the need to change himself to suit other people's preferences. His must have had to adapt to survive.

If MacGregor and Associates was any indication, Dane was surviving quite nicely. He'd achieved notable success. Or had he? If he still felt he had to be something he wasn't, his life must be full of frustration. And fear, Laurel remembered as she thought of their conversation last night at dinner....

HER NIGHT ALONE wasn't turning out to be as soothing as she'd expected. Even after dinner and a long soak in the tub, she was still thinking about Dane and her future with him.

Could she accept a man who was an admitted liar? How could she convince him that he didn't need to change himself for her? At a deeper level, she realized she was demanding a radical change. She wanted him to be himself, to be honest. And what was honesty? Something she'd always taken for granted.

She could have saved herself a lot of pain by lying. In her relationship with Alexander Fier, she could have pretended that she wasn't in love. But that wouldn't have altered the facts. He hadn't cared as deeply for her as she had for him. That was a simple shattering truth.

The similarities between Dane and her former lover still worried her. Both were businessmen. Both successful. Both claimed to love her. Unfortunately, Laurel thought with a shudder, there was no way of knowing whether Dane's love was true.

No money-back guarantee. Yet there was a deep vulnerability in Dane that had been missing in Alex. And the physical satisfaction she reached with Dane had been greater than she'd ever dreamed of experiencing.

She turned off the lights and slipped between the clean cotton sheets. The soft hum of the air conditioner permeated the silence. That was a part of urban life. If she turned off the air conditioner and opened the window, there would be traffic noises. For a time she would have to learn to live with the constant background of sound. While in the city, night would not be stars and velvet darkness. Instead there would be the sickly yellow glare of city lights. Maybe there was someplace on the outskirts of Atlanta where she could find a stream and tadpoles. But then she'd need a car. And an apartment. Furniture, newspaper subscription, telephone and clothes.

So many changes. Living in Atlanta and working for Meadow Flowers was like coming out of a dark cozy hibernation into the glare of daylight. For a while she expected to be blinking and disoriented, and there would surely be times, like tonight, when she would need to escape back into her warm safe cave.

But she'd taken the first tentative steps. Toward what? Where was she headed? There were so many risks, so much danger. She drifted into a deep sleep. Her last conscious thoughts were of Dane.

THE NEXT MORNING Laurel was raring to go. She bounded past the receptionist at MacGregor and Associates at a quarter past eight and went directly to Dane's office. Two raps and she flung the door open.

"Hi, there, boss man."

"Good morning, Ms Janeway. Would you please close the door." She did so, and he continued with a comical leer, "And get your body over here."

She perched on the edge of the desk before him and said, "You look tired."

"Sexual frustration does that to me."

"Aw, poor baby," she teased unsympathetically. "What's on our agenda for today?"

"Mort wants to see you as soon as possible, and Belinda has a schedule all made up. But first I have something for you."

"Animal, vegetable or mineral?"

"Definitely animal."

He came swiftly to his feet and swept her into a firm embrace, his mouth claiming hers in a fierce hard kiss. She felt the impact all the way down to her toes as she threw her arms around his neck and kissed back.

The friction of his body as he moved seductively against her created a falling sensation in her, not an uncontrolled plunge but a gentle floating. Drifting sensually she clung to him.

He leaned away and smacked his lips. "You taste even better than I remembered."

"Toothpaste."

"Haven't you had breakfast?"

"Only a few teaspoons of honey."

"Don't mention honey." He groaned and forcibly separated himself from her. "We'd better find Mort before I embarrass myself."

She caught his arm as he strode toward the door. Looking up into his red-rimmed eyes, she said, "You really do look exhausted."

"I couldn't sleep," he admitted. "My pillow wasn't an adequate substitute for you."

"I'd be complimented if I didn't feel so guilty."

"Guilty enough to remember your dinner reservation with me tonight? At my house."

She bobbed her head in happy assent. Together they went in search of Mort Joiner.

He wasn't hard to find. The sound of his voice led them to the photo studio, where Mort was lecturing an uninterested Freddy on the best way to photograph Laurel.

"Lots of teeth!" Mort shouted. "And hair. Definitely a sweep of hair across the face."

"Cleo wants long shots," Freddy drawled laconically.

"'Long shots'?" Mort scratched his head and brightened. "In the dress I designed? Perfect. Do you think we could work in a little teensy caption giving me credit for the clothes?"

"No captions," Dane said. "And no big toothy glamor poses. Where's Cleo?"

"At her desk, working on copy," Mort replied. "She said the slogan for this first layout would be something like: Meadow Flowers is for All of You."

Dane nodded. "First we establish product identification. Then we'll work out the specifics of tea, lotion and shampoo. All of You is the initial direction."

"'All of me'?" Laurel asked. "Exactly how much of me is going to be photographed?"

"Enough," Mort explained as he dragged her into the makeup room. "Enough so that women will want to look like you and men will want to look at you."

Casting a suspicious glance over her shoulder at Dane, Laurel allowed herself to be led into Mort's private laboratory.

The morning passed in an incredible flurry of activity. Laurel was made up, powdered and combed for one series of photographs. Wide-brimmed hats were slapped onto her head. She was bedecked with wildflowers, windblown by fans and swathed in an array of fabrics.

At one point she found herself arranged in a half-rising posture on a wrought-iron bench, bedazzled by Freddy's spotlights. She'd been told to focus on a wooden ladder that leaned in the corner. In her hand she held a single red rose that contrasted with her sleeveless white dress. Except for the incessant thrum of country-and-western music from Freddy's tape deck, there was a silence in the room.

Mort dashed forward to align the folds of her skirt and the drape of her hair. Slowly he backed away. "That's almost it," he whispered.

"Almost what?" she said in exasperation as Freddy's camera clicked one shot after another. "I've been poked and prodded and pushed into the most ridiculous postures. I've been told to purr and to growl and to laugh and to sneer. Maybe it would help if somebody told me what you're looking for."

Dane separated from the group of people behind the camera. He walked into the picture, the bright lights making a halo behind him. He knelt before her and took her hand in his. "The reason we haven't told you is that we're not sure. This is an experimental study. Later when we go over the proof sheets, some of the poses will stand out. One of them might even be perfect."

"How can you tell?"

"Instinct. I don't have Freddy's eye for composition or Mort's understanding of style, but I know when something is right. And I like the way you're looking right now."

"Thanks for explaining. An experiment . . . Now I understand why I've been feeling like a rat in a maze."

"Okay if I take over for a minute, Freddy?" At the other man's nod Dane said, "Take off your shoes and tuck your right foot underneath you, Laurel, please."

"Like this?" she said, assuming the pose.

"That's right. Now lean slightly back against the bench." Dane's voice was soft and cajoling as he set her shoulders and lifted her chin. "Now I want you to trail the rose along your cheek, but look at me and don't say, 'Cheese.'"

He skillfully guided her through a series of expressions and postures, and she followed all of his instructions precisely. As he came close to brush her hair behind her ear, she whispered, "I don't know if this is wise, allowing you to treat me like a mannequin."

His broad back shielding them from the rest of the people in the room, he gave her a look that could only be described as smoldering. "Believe me, Laurel, if I had my choice, this isn't what I'd be doing with your body."

Before she could respond verbally, he had moved away, and her intrigued half-smile burned an imprint on the film in Freddy's camera.

"All right, people." Dane turned and addressed them. "That's all for today. Tomorrow we go over the proofs and make some decisions."

Laurel had already made her decision. Tonight she would complete the sensual promise of that pose.

10

"IS IT A CONDOMINIUM? With lots of chrome and high-tech furniture?"

"No way," Dane said as he eased the BMW into traffic.

"Then your house has to be antebellum mansion. Am I right? Something out of *Gone With The Wind*, in which you can act out your Rhett Butler fantasies."

"Do I detect a note of eager anticipation? Even from a feminist like you? Well, I'm sorry, Scarlett. I don't own a mansion. But I might consider renting one if I could sweep you off your feet, carry you up a long staircase and ravish you to my heart's content."

Laurel snuggled back against the white leather upholstery and studied his profile. While the day-long photo session had left her feeling tired and limp, the work seemed to renew Dane. His dark eyes shone, and his dimpled smile revealed amusement at her guessing game.

"You can tell a lot about someone from where they live. Give me a clue. Do you entertain a lot?"

"Not in my home. My business parties are usually on a large scale requiring caterers and a restaurant."

"So it's a small place," she deduced. "A boat? Are there any houseboats around here?"

"Not in land-locked Atlanta. Though it's possible that someone might have a boat on the Chattahooches."

"An airplane hangar," she said quickly. "I'll bet you live at the airport. Or in a giant balloon. A dirigible?"

"Sorry to disappoint you, but my home is really rather conventional."

"It's not a tree house, is it?"

"Nope. I'm not Tarzan, Rhett or Captain Hook. Just a fairly conservative advertising man with simple tastes."

"Why is that hard for me to believe?" She leaned back in the seat once more and closed her eyes. "Maybe it's because you always seem to be playing a role—pilot, cowboy, Neanderthal, super-charged executive. I expect you to be flamboyant, larger than life."

"I do have a king-sized bed."

"A castle," she said dreamily. "You live in a vast Gothic castle where knights clank around in armor and giant mastiff dogs eat scraps from the roundtable. Like Sleeping Beauty's castle at Disneyland. Have you ever been to Disneyland?"

"Sure, when I was a kid. Mother and husband number two took me, and I got lost near the Matterhorn ride."

"I bet you lost yourself on purpose," she said. "My family went there when I was eight, and I remember wanting to stay forever."

"You're right." He chuckled ironically. "Anyplace was better than where I was living when I was ten years old."

"Do you want to tell me about it?"

"Not really, but I will. As part of our official get-to-know-each-other-better program, I promise to bare my sordid past. Right after dinner." He slowed the car and turned into a cul-de-sac. The street sign on the corner said Cynthia Drive. "Here we are, Laurel. We're home."

She saw a cedar A-frame house at the edge of a small forest. Though other homes were visible through the trees, the setting was secluded. He drove around a narrow cobblestone drive and parked in a rustic garage overgrown with honeysuckle vines.

Laurel felt a thrill of excitement. Though his home was a far cry from a mountain cabin, it was the closest she'd ever seen to one within a city's limits. She got out of the car and dashed across the cobblestone pavement.

The variety and proliferation of foliage astounded her. Vines and trees and brambles and a large strawberry patch covered the area in front of the house, shielding it from the street. She stood beside a tall shrub with shiny elliptical leaves. "This is a mountain laurel," she said. "Right here in your front yard. I can't believe it."

"It wasn't intentional," he assured her. "As you know, I'm not up on herbs and plants. The previous owner said the landscaping was specifically designed for a minimum of maintenance. All that's needed is an occasional picking of the berries. Which is fine with me, because that's about as far as my interest in gardening goes."

"I can see that," she said, yet her enthusiasm grew as she explored. "You are in definite need of pruning. This blueberry shrub is as tall as a tree. And you really should harvest the berries for jelly. I wonder if you could use these laurel leaves the same way you use bay leaves. They're in the same family, you know."

"But you're one of a kind." He stepped to her side and threw an arm around her shoulders for a fond hug. "I halfway expected you to tell me the place needed a woman's touch. But you want to reform me horticulturally."

"I'm not criticizing. I love it."

"Would you like to see the inside? Or would you rather forage for dinner?"

"Foraging is a perfectly respectable way to eat." She wrapped her arm around his torso. "But I am hungrier than berries would satisfy."

The interior of his A-frame gave an impression of spaciousness. An upstairs loft with cedar-rail banister overlooked the front room, which was open all the way to the beamed peak of the A. The front wall was almost all window from floor to ceiling. Dane's furniture was predictably large and masculine.

Dane led her up one stair, past a dining area and into the kitchen. "I'll cook," he announced. "How about a salad with crabmeat and a steak?"

"I'll skip the cow flesh, but the salad sounds great. I'll help."

Dane found lettuce, tomato, scallions and spinach in the refrigerator and pulled a fresh-frozen package of crab from the freezer. "I thought you said you weren't a vegetarian."

"I'm not. Steak just doesn't sound good." She nosed her way into the refrigerator. "What else have you got in here?"

"Not much."

"You can say that again."

"Not much."

"Ha, ha. What about pasta?" She turned to the nearly barren cupboards, happily finding a package of spaghetti. "Let's try this with crab sauce and the salad."

"Fine. I can handle that." He caught both her hands in his and pulled her away from the white ceramic tile countertops into the front room. "Congratulations, Laurel. You're going to learn something new about me. Even though I eat out a lot, I am a competent cook—not cordon bleu—but competent. You're my guest. I want you to relax, and I'll make dinner."

"Which shows how little you know about me. If there's something going on in the kitchen, I want to be there. Probably what motivates me is the suspicion that the cook is going to slip nitrates and preservatives into my food."

"You're not dressed to cook," he pointed out.

She looked down at the silky blue shirtwaist dress she'd worn from his office and agreed. "Mort would die if I spilled something on this, wouldn't he?"

"No, but he'd probably kill."

"Definitely not worth the risk. I'll have to change." She headed toward the circular wooden staircase in the corner. "Are the bedrooms up here? I'll find something."

"I'm glad to see you're not shy about barging into my bedroom."

She paused halfway up the staircase, aware that her behavior since they'd arrived didn't reflect the proper attitude of a houseguest. "I feel very much at home here, Dane. After all my guessing and carrying on, I haven't told you how lovely your home is."

"I was teasing, not fishing for compliments."

"Maybe it would be better if I sat quietly—" she descended a step "—and let you put on your show."

"I'd rather you didn't." He crossed the room, rested his hand over hers on the banister and gave a gentle squeeze. "I seem to get into trouble with you when I put on a show. Besides, I'm curious to see what kind of outfit you can find in my closet."

"I can be very inventive when I want to."

"Yes, Laurel," he said. The laugh lines around his eyes crinkled, and his slow grin hinted at a wealth of shared memories. "I know, honey."

She turned her hand beneath his, joining their palms. Then she raised his hand to her lips and kissed his fingertips. "This is what I want for us, Dane. Hugs and squeezes and a world of remembrance to build on."

Without elaboration, she climbed the circular stairs and found her way into his bedroom. Directly below her in the kitchen, he'd already started rattling pots. Her hand lingered on the light switch, admiring the view through his large uncurtained window. The forest behind the house reminded her of her own cabin, despite the vast difference between Rocky Mountain foliage and the verdant trees of Georgia.

Autumn must be beautiful in Dane's forest, she thought. Springtime, too, when the mountain laurel would blossom with white and pink flowers. She'd hate to miss spring. Or summer. Or winter. Maybe not winter, she amended. She'd miss the Colorado snowfall if she stayed here.

She cut short her musings and flicked on the light. Spring was still a long way off, but dinner was right downstairs, and she needed to change clothes. His closet formed part of a wood-paneled wall, and she slid open the doors, hoping to find an extra-large shirt.

Only three summer-weight suits were draped on wooden hangers beside a neat row of shirts. Very economical, she thought approvingly, for a man with such otherwise extravagant taste.

She fingered the expensive fabric and took note of the designer labels. Well, maybe not so economical, although this was a rather limited selection for a top executive. Perhaps his business wasn't as profitable as he'd led her to believe. Perhaps successful corporate president was just another of his images. Another deception.

Pushing the closet doors wide, she took inventory of the contents, feeling embarrassed about this affront to his privacy and even guiltier about her suspicions. At the same time she wanted to know—had to know more about him. Of course, the obvious solution would be to ask. She shook her head. What should she say? "I happened to notice that your closet isn't well stocked. Are you broke?"

That simply wouldn't do, but this couldn't possibly be his entire wardrobe. The leather jacket he'd had on when she'd first met him wasn't even here. Laurel flipped past a rack where striped and monochrome neckties hung in a color-coordinated row. Was there no clue to his personality in the display? Only that Dane was incredibly neat.

For the moment she gave up trying to solve the mystery, and feeling somewhat foolish, selected a Hawaiian print shirt, shed her dress and slipped into it. The long shirttails came almost to her knees. As she hung her silk dress beside his suits, she grinned. The soft feminine material contrasted with his stern, solid three-piece outfits, yet it looked as if it belonged there.

She padded barefoot across the hardwood floor into the adjoining bathroom. Everything was gleaming white and spotlessly clean. The sunken bathtub was round and exceptionally large. Here was where Dane could use a woman's touch, she thought. A few nice leafy plants and potpourri jars would make some homey clutter. There was nothing here but shaving cream, razor, shampoo and soap, the bare essentials. Even her bathroom at the motel had more character. The pristine room puzzled her, even though she acknowledged that men didn't appreciate the finer points of long soaks in the tub.

Laurel returned to the kitchen to find Dane cooking, a task he undertook with outright vigor. He was probably as successful in the kitchen as he seemed to be in all other endeavors. So why was she bent on nit-picking? Obviously the man was perfect.

Broccoli steamed. Pasta boiled. With sleeves rolled up, he stood before the stove, stirring a creamy roux for the crabmeat.

"How do you like the outfit?" she asked, striking a slouching model's pose. "Do you think I'll start a trend in oversized Hawaiian shirts?"

"It's definitely hot," he said, pretending to scrutinize her through the lens of a camera. "But I don't think I'm ready to share you with the rest of the market. Nope, I'm not. Those legs are for my eyes only."

"Some entrepreneur you are. I thought you could sell anything."

"I can. The secret is that I keep the best for myself."

"Is there anything I can do to help?"

"You make the salad," he said, nodding toward the sink, where the fresh-washed ingredients lay beside a large wooden serving bowl.

"I want to compliment you on the tidiness of your bedroom closet," she said as she tore into the lettuce. "Do you have a cleaning lady?"

"A cleaning person, you sexist female. He comes in once a week for the major scrubbing, but I admit to being somewhat fanatical about cleanliness. I used to drive my mother crazy with my precision arrangement of magazines on the coffee table—a fanned-out display with one inch of cover showing on each."

"You're kidding."

"Not a bit. I'd line my sneakers up in a row with the laces tied to exactly the same length on each shoe. When we had a maid, she was expressly forbidden to enter my room."

"I suppose that's better than throwing your dirty socks and underwear around the room." Laurel opened a drawer to look for a paring knife and chuckled. "This is ridiculous, Dane. There's nothing in here but a box of matches."

"Of course not. That's the match drawer. Cutlery is one drawer to the right."

The paring knife was easy to find in the neat arrangement, and Laurel began slicing tomatoes. Through the window over the sink, she could see the trees behind the house. The pattern and variety of leaves seemed in delightful disarray.

"I'm not so exacting anymore," Dane went on.

"What caused you to change?"

"Growing up. Maybe because my early life was fairly chaotic, I needed to impose order whenever I could. We moved a lot, but I always kept my bedroom, drawers and closets as much the same as possible. When I started spending more time away from home, the neatness lost its importance. Now it's just a habit."

Her curiosity about his childhood had mounted to a suspenseful level, but she figured it would take careful and persistent probing to draw him out. Whenever he mentioned his early years, he did so only in passing. He offered brief comments that were not meant to be followed up or explained.

"This is almost ready," he said, removing the pot from the stove and adding the crabmeat. "How's the salad coming?"

"Do you mind if I leave the skin on these carrots? They really are more nutritious that way."

"Sure, I love eating dirt."

"I'll scrub them," she assured him. "It's ridiculous what people do to vegetables. After all the peeling, boiling and seasoning, the taste is ruined, and the healthful benefits are almost nil."

"How about some carrot-scrubbing music?"

He went to the stereo and arranged a stack of records on the turntable. The mellow seductive voice of William Ackerman filled the room, and Laurel sighed. This house, the trees and the music lulled her into a contented state.

"Maybe your neat habits are inherited," she said. "Is your mother a tidy person?"

"Physically she is. Very neat, clean and attractive. And our houses were always well tended. But her thoughts are unbelievably jumbled. She can forget what she was going to say before she's ended the sentence, but remembers every detail of some meaningless incident that occurred years before."

"Is she in good health?"

"She's not senile, if that's what you mean. She's one of those people who always claim to be on the verge of a nervous breakdown, but never actually collapse."

He left the sauce on a low flame and gathered dishes to set the table. "I'd have to say that the most consistent feature of my mother's behavior when I was growing up was the frequency with which she changed husbands."

"What about you? Aren't you a constant in her life? No matter what else changes, she always has a son."

"That never occurred to me. And to be quite honest, I'd rather not think of the mother-son relationship that way."

He laid two places at the table, taking an overlong time to set the silverware. His voice was almost inaudible as he continued. "It makes me feel too responsible."

While they finished preparations for dinner and brought the food to the table, Laurel turned over his comments in her mind. Certainly his childhood had had an effect on his behavior as an adult, but she couldn't decide quite how all these bits and pieces interconnected. His life was like a road map with many divergent routes and an unmarked destination.

While he gallantly held her chair, she took her place at the round glass-topped table and tried to invent another question that would lead him to reveal the connections.

Dane poured the wine. They clinked glasses. Their eyes met, locking in a poignant regard. All her questions took on new importance. When she gazed into his eyes, she found herself hoping this was a man she might spend a lifetime with, that she might see those crinkles around his eyes deepen and watch his thick brown hair turn snowy white.

A brief encounter would be unsatisfying and painful. She had to know him, all about him. For better or worse.

Laurel took a sip, set down her glass and said, "I've been sitting here trying to think of some way to manipulate you into telling me about your childhood."

"Have you?"

"And that's just plain silly. I'm not like that. When I want to know something, I ask. You must be having more of an effect on me than I realized."

"I have noticed some changes. You're not as cantankerous as when you first came here."

"But more suspicious. I'm almost ashamed to tell you, but I don't want to be a sneak." She took a deep breath. "I went through your closet upstairs."

"Oh, no!" he gasped in mock horror. "Did I forget to hide the girlie magazines?"

"Be serious, Dane. That was a terrible thing for me to do. Nosy and pushy, and I had no business drawing weird conclusions because you only have three suits."

"'Conclusions'?"

"I stupidly deduced that your business was probably bankrupt because you didn't have more clothes."

"Dead wrong."

"I know. My peanut-sized brain couldn't come up with a plausible explanation, though."

"Well, if you must know, most of my winter clothes are in storage."

He concentrated on his salad, picking through the lettuce with his fork until he found a carrot slice. His eyes were averted, making it impossible for her to read his expression. When he looked up and saw her watching him, he casually continued, "I have a condo near the office where I keep my other clothes."

"Why did you hesitate?" she asked with frank curiosity. "Is there something else you're not telling me?"

"Possibly," he admitted. "I'm not sure what you want to hear."

"Everything. I want every little detail. I want the complete unabridged truth about Dane MacGregor."

"We always seem to come back to the same place. The cold hard facts, ma'am, nothing but the facts. You know, Laurel, I think honesty is a highly overrated part of our relationship. Sometimes when you care deeply for someone, a small deception is kinder than the truth."

"That's where we differ." She twirled her pasta around her fork. "I don't see how any kind of sincere relationship can exist without trust. And trust goes hand in hand with honesty."

"Once I saw a hypnotist," he said. "He selected volunteers from the audience and asked for their trust. After it was given, he mesmerized those people into oinking like pigs and singing arias and tap dancing."

"So?"

"The trust came first, given freely because they expected to have a good time. Then he worked his magic. I think we're like that, Laurel. If you'd only forget all your suspicions, trust freely, we could relax and enjoy ourselves."

"Oinking like a pig is fun?"

"Trust me."

She thought for a moment. Dane had touched—ever so lightly—on the source of conflict within her. Her natural inclination was to trust everyone, to assume no one meant her harm. As she gazed at him she wanted to trust, to give him all that was inside her.

Yet he'd misled her too often. From his bravado when they had first met to the latest deception about Ultra Taste, he seemed compelled to stop just short of the truth, and she couldn't understand why.

"First, let's hear all about your childhood," she insisted, dismissing his request for blind trust.

"Okay, Laurel. I guess I'll just have to come clean." He pursed his lips and squinted up at the ceiling in supposedly intense thought. "I robbed my first bank when I was six and a half, just tall enough to peak over the teller's counter. Then, of course, there was my first job wrestling killer pythons. And the years—when I was ten or eleven—that I spent in the French Foreign Legion."

"Dane! Would you stop."

"I'm making a point here. My life was nothing unusual. I was just like everybody else. No thrills and chills. I was an average kid. Middle to upper-middle class."

"Where did you live? What part of the country?"

"In the exotic wilds of the Midwest. Chicago, Des Moines and Kansas City. I'm sure it comes as no surprise to you that I was always a city kid—more precisely, a suburb kid. From age ten onward I lived in Detroit."

"I consider that fairly exciting," she said, stabbing at her salad. "I lived in Denver all my life. Every summer and holiday we vacationed at my grandparents' cabin."

He savored a bite of the spaghetti with crab sauce. "This is pretty good, if I do say so myself. Wait until you taste my omelettes tomorrow morning."

"Tell me about your father," she persisted.

"He smoked a pipe, and he was some sort of traveling salesman. Of course, I didn't know that at the time. He and my mother were divorced when I was five. All I understood was that he took a lot of long trips, and then he left for good. For some reason I associate my father with autumn. I remember that we used to play catch with a red rubber football. In a park when the trees were turning orange and yellow. And then we'd walk home and rake the leaves into piles and burn them."

He paused, took a sip of wine and continued, "I never hated my father for divorcing my mother. I missed him a lot, but he managed to stay in fairly close contact even when we moved to other cities. He was there for me when I needed him, and I think that over the years I've made him proud."

"I'm sure you have. No one would argue with your many successes, Dane."

"No one but you." He reached across the table and laid his hand on top of hers. "Why? Why is it so hard for you to love me?"

His touch melted her resistance. He was asking her a simple question. Certainly she should give him an equally direct answer. She was supposed to be the straightforward Laurel Janeway, a paragon of honesty.

"I'm afraid to trust you," she blurted out.

The raw pain in his eyes sparked an echoing response in her. It would have been kinder to lie, she realized, to ignore her misgivings and tell him how deeply she cared. She held his hand tightly.

"Remember your story about the hypnotist?" she asked. He nodded.

"Those people gave their trust because there was no risk involved. They knew the man on stage wasn't going to harm them. Emotional commitment to another person isn't so easy. You've already deceived me, Dane. And I'm scared. I don't want to be hurt."

"I'd never hurt you, Laurel. I love you."

"Then why do you deceive me?"

"I assume you're referring to our misunderstanding about Ultra Taste."

He withdrew his hand, and she felt abandoned, as if cut loose to fend for herself in an unfriendly atmosphere. She mustered all her courage and plunged forward. These bones of contention had to be cleared away. "And your supposedly special gift of flowers. And the basic fact that you led me to believe my recipes would be the focus of Meadow Flowers. And the auction. And the way you lured me to Atlanta."

"Hasn't it all turned out for the best?" he protested. "You approve of the focus of the advertising campaign, don't you?"

"Yes, I do."

"We're here together. We've shared so much already. I might be guilty of little white lies, but none of them have been designed to hurt you."

"The end doesn't justify the means, Dane." She rose from the table and walked stiffly into the large open front room.

"You never would have left your mountains if I'd been completely honest, would you?"

"I might have." In a very small voice she added, "From the first moment I saw you, I knew I cared."

"That wasn't my impression," he said. "If I recall correctly, you stomped off in a huff."

"You're right. I objected to your macho posturing. Remember what you said? You'd just come through a crash-landing that terrified me, and you said, 'Piece of cake. Sorry to drop in on you like this.'"

"A harmless joke."

"No." She pivoted to face him. "It wasn't a joke. It was part of this image you keep projecting, and it wasn't the truth. You were afraid. Any normal person would have been panic-stricken."

He jumped to his feet, came to her in swift strides and held both her arms in an iron grip. "Sure, I was scared. Every time I get in a plane, every time I race, I'm scared out of my mind. Does it make you feel good to hear that?"

"Yes, because it's honest."

His eyes were coal black, smoldering with rage. She could feel his tension.

"Dane, you don't have to be someone else for me. You don't have to be a daredevil or a successful executive. You don't have to dress up in costumes. There doesn't need to be a scenario. I don't care if you drive a BMW or a broken-down heap. You don't have to prove anything to me. I love you."

With fierce strength he clutched her to him. His heart pounded like a jackhammer against her as she clung to him, repeating over and over in a soothing chant, "I love you, Dane. Love you. Love you."

His tension gradually ebbed. The strong arms that held her loosened their grip. He stroked the length of her long blond hair, his fingers smoothing the thick silken strands. When she looked into his eyes, she saw that anger had been replaced by another passion, equally strong but not frightening. There was a purity to his gaze, an undeniable honesty as he said, "I love you, Laurel."

Still cradling her against him, he crossed the few steps to the center of the room. Directly beneath the high arch of the A in the ceiling, he unfastened the buttons on the oversized Hawaiian shirt she wore and slipped the brilliant fabric off her shoulders.

"Shouldn't we turn off the lights?" she asked. "There are so many windows."

"No one can see in." He went to the front door and flicked one switch that doused all the lamps on the lower floor of the house. Moonlight shone through the high front windows, and she could see trees outside etched in blue shadows. "But I'll humor you."

She went to the window and touched the glass.

When he came to her again in the darkness, he was naked. His flesh was warm against her back as he fastened his arms around her. The rough prickling of the hair on his chest contrasted with the cool smooth glass.

"This view must be beautiful in springtime," she said, "when the laurel is in bloom."

"Would you stay here with me and find out?"

"Move in?"

"Please, Laurel. I can't imagine this house without you."

She turned within the circle of his embrace. Such a major decision should not be taken lightly, yet Laurel knew this moment was as inevitable as their lovemaking. When she had left Colorado, she had made a commitment to their relationship. One step after another, she would head down the path she'd chosen. At each divergent fork in the road she needed to pause for only an instant before her instincts dictated the direction.

Though she could postpone the inevitable, her route was already set, and there was no reason to wait. "I'll stay with you."

She confirmed her words with a kiss, standing on tiptoe and joining her mouth with his. Her tongue tasted white wine on his lips and she reveled in the sweeter flavor inside.

Giving of herself meant partaking of the essence of him, his love, his laughter. So many things about him were good to love.

She rested her cheek on his chest, adoring the heaving motion of his breathing and the tickling of his hair. He seemed almost to be trembling. Was it possible that she inspired such powerful emotion?

"Thank you, Laurel," he whispered, his hands gliding down the gentle slope of her back. "Thank you for this chance."

She looked up, finding perfect masculine beauty in Dane's high cheekbones and rugged jaw. The incandescent blue of moonlight dramatically highlighted his strong features and glistened on the dark hair swept back from his forehead.

Her hands crept slowly up his chest, over his collarbone and met around his neck. She held his face in both hands, overwhelmed by the wonder of his love for her.

She could almost have stood there forever, suspended in time and space. They stood twined together, a marvelous sculpture of living stone, silhouetted against the forest beyond the window.

Yet her desire for him was an active force. His hard male body demanded a response she was eager to give. She slid her hands down his body, feeling his vibrant flesh harden and tingle beneath her gentle caress. She traced the pattern of dark hair down his torso and fondled him intimately.

"Not yet," he gasped. "We have all the time in the world."

He nuzzled the top of her head. His fingers teased the tight buds of her breasts, bringing a pleasured moan from her lips. He went on his knees before her, adoring every inch of her flesh with his lips and tongue and fingers. When he found the center of her desire, she backed toward the window.

Her knees were too weak for her to stand, so she leaned against the hard glass. The cold surface heightened the flaming excitement that engulfed her body. She heard herself breathing his name as she sank to the carpet and pulled him over her.

"Now, Dane. I can't wait anymore."

His first thrust released her into a buzzing ecstasy of delight. Each stroke drove her higher until she'd passed the boundaries of moonlight and wispy clouds and flown over the planets into a dark and wonderful beyond.

Afterward they sprawled together, exhausted. Vaguely she heard him mumbling something about food.

"What did you say?" she asked.

"Are you hungry?"

She laid a hand on her stomach and considered.

"I'm hungry," he said.

"And that's the difference between men and women," she said lazily. "I'm floating around in the stratosphere, and you're thinking about food."

"You wanted me to be honest," he reminded her.

"So I did. And I do." She dragged herself to a sitting position. "We didn't finish dinner."

"But it's cold. Cold pasta tastes like worms." He planted a quick kiss on her lips and headed toward the kitchen. "You stay here. I'll see what else I can find to eat."

She heard him stumble over a chair as he crossed the room. After a few seconds of banging and clanging in the kitchen, he shouted, "Laurel? Laurel, is it okay if I turn on a light?"

"Of course it is." She rolled over to her stomach and shielded her eyes with her arms. "It's your house."

The light went on. She could feel the glare, and almost immediately he was beside her. "You don't mean that, do you?"

"Mean what?" She squinted up at him.

"That this is my house. It's our house, isn't it? You are going to be living here, aren't you?"

"Of course, I am." She clambered to her feet and found the Hawaiian shirt. "And I suggest that you put on your trousers, or we're going to scandalize any neighbor who happens to be out walking the dog past this window."

"I told you before, you can't see in this window from the street."

"Be civilized, Dane," she said, buttoning the bright shirt. "If you're going to be cooking, you shouldn't be naked. It's unsanitary."

"All right. If you insist." He slipped into his trousers, then grinned. "Do you know what's ironic about all this?"

"How many guesses do I get?"

"None. Because I'm going to tell you. When I dragged you out here from the mountains, part of the express purpose was a make over. I thought I was going to change you."

"Did you want me to change?"

"Honestly?"

"I can take it," she teased, grabbing a pillow from the sofa and holding it over her head in a threatening pose.

"I did." She fired the pillow, and he deflected it easily. "Only in superficial ways. When I first saw you I told myself you could be a knockout with properly plucked eyebrows and a dash of lipstick."

"Well?" she asked, batting her newly dyed eyelashes. "What do you think?"

"Apart from minuscule daubs of makeup, I think you're not going to change one bit. And that's the irony. I'm the one who needs to be different."

"Not different," she said. "All you need to be is yourself."

Dane grinned and headed back toward the refrigerator. Be himself? If she only knew what she was asking would she be so anxious for him to change?

11

DURING THE NEXT two and a half months, Dane and Laurel were almost constantly in each other's company. They lived in the same house, worked in the same office and traveled on the same business junkets. Yet they shared very little time alone.

Their privacy was sacrificed for Meadow Flowers; the launch of the advertising campaign was tremendously successful. Meadow Flowers products—shampoo, body lotion and herbal tea—were massively distributed through the Ultra Taste system. Print advertising, two television promos and personal appearances by Laurel Janeway convinced the public to try Meadow Flowers. The quality of the products ensured repeat sales.

As a model Laurel would never be better than average. She simply couldn't project the combination of chic and sex that would prove seductively persuasive. Long exhausting photo sessions only produced different angles of the same woman whom Mort had described as a colorless blob.

Her image, however, was both a personal and business triumph. People instinctively trusted her. In a whirlwind cross-country promotional tour, interviewers were impressed with her knowledge of herbal products and her straightforward style. She received stacks and stacks of fan mail—so much that Belinda hired a secretary to help her process the many requests for advice on natural beauty and health aids.

Only with Dane's steadfast support did Laurel manage to survive the overpowering crush of attention. He was always there for her, knowing exactly when to call an end to an interview and when to insist that she rise to the occasion.

He had been wonderfully undemanding. She couldn't count the number of times she'd fallen asleep in his arms, too drained to even attempt lovemaking. And there had been other nights when he had sensed and fulfilled their mutual need, skillfully guiding her to the peak of ecstasy.

She was thinking about all those times as she sat before the tall front windows of their house. Outside, the trees had lost the blazing crimson and gold of autumn, and the bare branches stretched tall fingers into a cloudy November sky. There was a portent of stormy weather.

Dane had already left for the office, and Belinda would be arriving soon to transport Laurel to a speaking engagement at a craft fair. Laurel was dressed and waiting, savoring an unaccustomed quiet private moment. A steaming mug of freshly brewed Meadow Flowers sassafras tea was in her hand. She was smiling peacefully.

Life felt very very good these days. Despite the constant rushing and hype, Laurel was happy. The direction of the Meadow Flowers advertising campaign emphasized all the values she believed in. Of course, hype and glitter were part of promotion, but she sincerely believed her work was akin to a public service. The Meadow Flowers campaign was educating consumers about the natural solutions to health and beauty problems. The bonus was that Ultra Taste was already researching alternative recipes for their sugar-coated cereal products. And the conglomerate was now considering including her own recipes in the product line.

Professionally, she was proud of her efforts.

And then there was Dane. She sighed deeply as she thought of him—the most handsome, the funniest, the sexiest man in the world. Though living together had not always been a romantic idyll, they had discovered an easy compatibility despite their differences.

They developed a pattern of his, hers and ours. Some of "his" time was still devoted to competitive sports in which she had little interest, such as tennis and racquet ball at the local athletic club. Fortunately he hadn't even mentioned stock-car racing or ultralights to her. Her time was spent pruning the forest outside the house and introducing a mob of houseplants to the bathroom. Their time together was spent reading, talking, cooking and watching bad, old monster movies on television.

Laurel appreciated his tidiness, especially when it came to dividing household chores, and she thought that during their time together his tendency to mislead others had lessened, almost ceased completely. With one exception.

Their living arrangement had been kept secret from everyone but Belinda. Dane had rationalized that their personal life was strictly that, and there was no need to get the office gossiping or to upset the Meadow Flowers people. Though she'd agreed, she had warned him that she wouldn't lie. If anyone asked directly, she would answer truthfully.

Strangely, that had never occurred. There were luncheons and speeches and question-and-answer sessions, but Laurel wasn't close to anyone but Belinda. No one else had inquired about where she lived. All her phone calls were screened, and her mail came directly to the office. With her hectic schedule, Laurel had neither time nor inclination to establish a social network. She hoarded every free moment to spend with Dane.

Through the tall window of the A-frame, she watched as Belinda parked on the edge of the cobblestone driveway and unfolded her lanky frame from the shiny Ford Escort, part of a new fleet of economy cars leased by MacGregor and Associates.

Belinda sauntered up the two stairs to the house. The tall elegant black woman never looked frazzled no matter how frantic the schedule.

Laurel opened the door and glared disapprovingly at Belinda's furry white jacket.

"Don't worry, honey," Belinda said. "It's fake."

"Aren't you hot with such a heavy jacket?" As Belinda strode past her into the house, Laurel paused in the doorway. The damp scent of late autumn hung in the air, but the sun was shining and the weather was crisp.

"I'm a warm-blooded woman," Belinda informed her. "Soon as the temperature drops to sixty, I'm chilled."

"I thought you modeled in New York. How did you survive those winters?"

"In misery."

"Do we have time for tea?"

"None for me, but you go ahead." Belinda slipped the fake fur coat off her shoulders and arranged herself on the sofa beside the window. "These craft things always run late, anyway. You're going to love this one. The honored speaker is one of those old Foxfire mountain men who's probably going to tell us dumb city folk how we can live off pine cones and still have all our own teeth at age seven hundred and seven."

"Do I detect a note of sarcasm?" Laurel sat in a chair opposite the sofa. "Is all this back to nature getting to you?"

"No offense, honey. Those Blue Ridge mountain men smell like they've been sleeping with raccoons. But I'm not complaining. Atlanta in the winter is better than New York."

"Is that why you left? The weather?" Laurel gazed into her mug of tea. "I'm sorry, Belinda. I didn't mean to pry. It's just that you're always so chic and beautiful. I can't believe you're not one of the top models."

"Two years ago in the Big Apple, I wasn't exactly gorgeous. Hasn't Dane told you?"

Laurel shook her head.

"If you want to hear my sad story, you'd better promise that it goes no further."

"I wouldn't dare double-cross you," Laurel said wryly. "Especially since you know all my secrets."

"I do?" the other asked, aghast. "Like what?"

"For instance, you're the only one who knows that I occasionally sneak a nonherbal Hershey bar on the road. And you alone know that I live with Dane. That's not common knowledge around the office, is it?"

"Nobody's heard it from me. Of course, any fool with two eyes in his head can see that you two are in love. I don't see why Dane doesn't up and marry you. Make an honest woman of you."

"Interesting choice of phrase. If we're not married does that make me a dishonest woman?"

"I'll tell you, honey. Those legal words on a scrap of paper do make a difference. I don't think it's about honesty. Or about love. It's about commitment. For better or for worse. Believe me, child. When you're legally married you learn to put up with a whole lot before you walk out the door."

Laurel knew she was right about the importance of commitment in a relationship. Dane had proposed marriage more than once, and Laurel's tentative acceptances always deferred the wedding date. Someday—after the first excitement of the Meadow Flowers campaign died down, she had told him. Or when the mountain laurel came into bloom.

In less romantic moments she had also told him the truth. Though she was ready to commit herself totally for the moment or for the day, she still lacked the absolute trust necessary for a permanent arrangement. And in her eyes marriage was forever.

She finished the last sip of sassafras tea, set down the mug and yawned. "We've gotten off the subject, Belinda. You were going to tell me a sad story."

"In the car, honey. You've finished your tea."

They drove through Atlanta streets that were now pleasantly familiar to Laurel. She had watched the seasons change and felt more comfortable with the city. The leaves had made a beautiful transition from green to an incredible show of color, and now to brown. Plant life was in the dormant stage, quiet and waiting for rebirth.

While they rode, Belinda talked.

"A couple of years back, in New York, my marriage fell to pieces. Which was okay, because that marriage was mostly the 'for worse' part of my wedding vows. The problem was that I was pregnant at the time. Oh, how I wanted that baby, but I also needed a bigger income, since my do-nothing husband had left me flat broke. So I kept dieting and taking jobs and not telling anybody for fear I wouldn't get assignments."

"Wasn't there somebody you could turn to?"

"I'm sure there was, but I wasn't thinking straight. It just seemed like it was me and my baby all alone. In my fourth month, I miscarried."

"Oh, Belinda. I'm so sorry."

"I mourned that baby even though it hadn't even been born. And I went a little crazy. Started taking drugs to lose weight, then eating like a horse in spite of the drugs. Honey, I was a sorry mess. I probably would have killed myself if it hadn't been for Dane."

"How did he get involved?"

"My sister does some modeling here in town, and she talked to the man and told him all about me, since he does take trips to New York often. She asked him to talk to me. Next thing you know, here's this big handsome dude standing on my doorstep and telling me it's time to come home. No two ways about it. I put up one real nasty fight, but he got me here. Back into the arms of my family. Their love—and his kindness—made me well again."

Laurel felt a surge of pride in Dane. What a wonderful healing thing for him to do! To help another human so much. And he'd never mentioned it to her.

"I'm not the only one," Belinda said. "Maybe I was the worst case of down and out, but Dane has helped a lot of people."

"Mort after his divorce?"

"Yes, ma'am. And Carlos the stock boy. Dane MacGregor is a good man—the best. Of course, you know about Thanksgiving. That's coming up in just a couple of weeks."

"No, I know of nothing special." She'd hoped to invite him to Denver so that he could meet her parents, but those plans hadn't been confirmed. "What happens on Thanksgiving?"

"I better not say anything. I don't want to let the cat out of the bag if he's planning some kind of surprise."

"Tell me," Laurel demanded. "Or else I'll announce at this fair that Meadow Flowers shampoo makes your hair fall out."

"Don't you get feisty with me, young lady." Belinda pulled into a parking spot outside a huge church where a wedding party had gathered. "Let Dane tell you in his own way."

"What are we doing here?" Laurel asked. "I thought we were going to a craft fair."

"We are." Belinda pointed to the church annex where large attractive posters announced the pre-Christmas craft fair. "What's the matter with you, girl? We've done fairs and meetings in churches before."

Laurel couldn't drag her attention away from the happy young bride and groom. The young woman hiked up the long white satin folds of her dress to dive into the back seat of a limousine. Her face was flushed, radiant. Her groom proudly held her arm. They looked so very young.

Laurel sighed. "There goes an honest woman."

"Don't look old enough to get married, do they?"

"Too old. Too young. Maybe it's never the right time."

As they walked into the fair, Laurel thought about marriage to Dane. It was the next logical step along their shared path.

They had already gone through the uncomfortably polite stage of getting to know each other and adjusting their habits. She had learned to line up her shoes neatly on racks in the bottom of the closet. He'd given up his morning coffee in favor of tea. Why not, indeed.

In the large open room of the church annex, booths were arranged in rows. There was quite a crowd in attendance, probably two or three hundred not including the craftspeople. At the far end of the room was a stage where a dais had been set.

Belinda led them unerringly past the homemade baked goods and the professional pottery to the Meadow Flowers booth. One of the nutritionists from Meadow Flowers manned the front, and Dane lounged in a folding chair at the rear.

Laurel's eyes brightened when she caught sight of him. He looked the same as always. His three-piece suit, navy blue, was immaculate. His thick brown hair was combed back from his forehead. And yet she was seeing him differently. For the first time she saw him through the eyes of a young bride.

There seemed to be a special glow surrounding him. The noises of the crowd faded to a monotonous buzz. When he spoke she heard only his voice.

"You're lovely today, Laurel. The pale blue silk matches your eyes."

"Thank you, Dane. I didn't expect you at this show."

"Media," he said, pointing to a bored-looking reporter and photographer. "They're from New Orleans, only in town for the day, and I thought we could give them an exclusive interview after your speech."

"Fine with me."

In her floating love-dazed mood, Laurel would have agreed to anything—a belly dance, a moon walk—anything. She even smiled at Cleo.

Cleo greeted her with a typical caustic comment. "My, my, don't we look airy today."

"Do we? I hadn't noticed."

Laurel wrinkled her nose slightly. Even in this crowd Cleo's perfume was overwhelming, and the surreptitious glances she aimed at the men from New Orleans told an interesting tale. Poor Cleo, Laurel thought. The woman might by a copywriting genius, but she certainly lacked subtlety. In honor of her own happy mood, Laurel decided to be generous.

"I like your suit. Is it new?"

"Yes." Cleo's heavily made up eyes narrowed suspiciously. "I have a lunch date."

This was the closest the two women had ever come to friendliness, and Laurel was careful not to smile back at the New Orleans men, who were giving her appreciative grins. Over the past couple of months she'd become expert at tactful put-downs. She didn't want to ruin anything that Cleo might have going.

"When am I supposed to do the interview?" Laurel asked.

"Right after your speech."

"I'll try to keep it short."

Laurel coasted through the barrage of autographs, handshakes and questions. When it came time for her to speak from the podium, she slipped her arm through Dane's and asked, "Will you escort me?"

"I'd be delighted." He looked surprised, but pleased. Halfway to the stage he asked, "Are you up to something? Is there some devious scheme up your blue silk sleeve?"

"Why would you think that?" she said innocently, glancing over her shoulder to confirm that the men from New Orleans had seen and noted her obvious attachment to Dane. There should be no doubt that she was a woman in love, especially not when the role was so natural.

They reached the podium, and the speakers made a place for Dane on the stage. After an introduction, Laurel stepped up to the microphone. Her quick speech on the natural benefits of Meadow Flowers herbal products flowed glibly off her tongue, after which she asked for questions.

First came a question about the value of wild herbs versus those that were home grown.

"Wild herbs are supposed to be more potent for medicinal use, and more flavorful," Laurel said. "However, since it isn't possible to manufacture a product using only wild herbs without denuding the forests, Meadow Flowers cultivates their own gardens and adjusts their recipes accordingly."

She pointed to a woman in the front row, who stood and asked, "Is the gentleman who escorted you to the stage Dane MacGregor?"

"Yes, he is," Laurel said. "Please stand up, Mr. Mac-Gregor. He's the president of the company—MacGregor and Associates—in charge of the Meadow Flowers advertising."

"I have a question for him," the woman said. "Are you still going to have that stock-car race on Thanksgiving for the FPA? And will you be driving in the race?"

Laurel backed away from the microphone to allow Dane to answer the question. She felt as if her rosy cloud had suddenly evaporated.

A car race on Thanksgiving? What was the FPA?

"Yes," he said. "To both of your questions. And thank you for giving me the opportunity to publicize this event. Every Thanksgiving I sponsor an afternoon of stock-car racing. All proceeds from the gate and the entrants' fees go to the Foster Parents of Atlanta."

There was a smattering of applause.

"Now I hate to brag, but I've won the final race for two years running. And I hope to win this year so I can donate my winnings to the FPA and maybe improve the benefits for all the families who are helped by this worthy organization."

Laurel returned to the microphone to field questions. Was ginseng good for arthritis? How do you get rid of warts? When do you harvest angelica?

She'd heard it all before and answered by rote, amazed that she'd developed the capability to perform when her heart wasn't in it. The relationship she had imagined with Dane seemed to be slipping away. He still didn't trust her. Otherwise he would have told her about the stock-car race. They could have discussed it.

She wanted to escape this place, to be alone until the ache of disillusionment had abated. But that sort of behavior wouldn't suit her image.

Her session was over, and the Blue Ridge mountain man was introduced. Laurel took her seat on the opposite side of the stage from Dane, neatly crossed her ankles and folded her hands in her lap. With eyes firmly fixed on the scruffy back of the mountain man, she gave the impression of polite attention—so important for the image.

Yet her mind was far away. She'd been a pawn. Very obediently she'd done everything he'd wanted, expecting some compromise in return. She had trusted him. Why was he still working these deceptions?

Her eyes wandered, and she spied Belinda in the crowd. What would she say? What would her advice be? Laurel blinked once and looked away. She knew the answer to those questions. Belinda would tell her she was overreacting. She'd say, "Honey, Dane is a good man. Let him make an honest woman of you."

The mountain man had apparently made a joke, because everyone was laughing. Laurel trained her lips into a wide grin.

Was she making too much of this stock-car race? After all, it was for a good cause. But that wasn't the issue. Dane knew how much she despised his racing and flying and daredevil stunts. And he'd given them up. Or so she had thought. Maybe he was sky diving on the afternoons she thought he was at the office.

And why hadn't he told her? Maybe if they had talked it over—if he had been honest with her—she would have found a way to compromise. The race was only a couple of weeks away. Had he expected to hide it from her?

Everyone was laughing again, and Laurel joined in. Why not? She was so confused that she didn't know what was funny or serious.

The speech was over, and she applauded along with everyone else. Before she could rise to her feet, Dane appeared and took her hand. "I'm sorry, Laurel. Please believe me. There wasn't any way I could get out of this race."

"The race itself doesn't matter, Dane. What hurts is that you didn't trust me enough to tell me about it. Why?"

"I didn't want you to be angry. I was waiting for the right moment."

The right time. Less than an hour ago she had thought it was the right time to make a commitment. But now?

"Excuse me, Dane." It was Belinda. "Laurel needs to do her interview with these men from New Orleans."

She separated them neatly, leading the unprotesting Laurel through a side exit away from the crowd. She stopped next to the car and looked down into Laurel's glazed blue eyes. "What's the matter, honey?"

"Thanksgiving. He didn't even mention the race. I know it sounds dumb to object to a charity event. But he knows that I hate race cars and ultralights." She spread her hands wide, trying to contain the confusion that threatened to spill from her. "If only he'd told me, it would have been all right."

"It's not dumb for you to be upset. I didn't know it was so important to you. But Dane knows, doesn't he?" Laurel nodded. "I'd say the dumb one is about six feet two inches tall and wearing a navy-blue suit. It's hard for him to trust people, Laurel. All I can say is be patient."

Hard for him to trust her? Laurel didn't understand. She had never deceived him. Why shouldn't he believe her?

There wasn't a chance for Belinda to explain further, because Cleo's voice rang out from the end of the sidewalk.

"There you are!" Her arm was linked with the reporter from New Orleans in what Laurel considered a sickening parody of the bridal couple she'd seen earlier.

She braced herself for an interview. Since these reporters had already heard her expert's speech on herbs, they now concentrated on "up-close and personal" aspects of Laurel Janeway, media star.

She tersely answered their questions, the same questions she'd heard a hundred times before. Yes, she used Meadow Flowers products. Yes, she had lived alone for several months in a mountain cabin in Colorado. No, she didn't follow any special sort of diet but recommended exercise and healthy food.

Then came the surprise question. "Is it true that you and Dane MacGregor are getting married?"

"Who told you that?" Laurel glared at Cleo.

"Lucky guess. Is it?"

"I'm feeling rather tired," she said. "I appreciate your time and interest in Meadow Flowers, but you will have to excuse me. Miss Belinda Crawford will answer any more of your questions."

She held out her hand for the keys to the Ford Escort, which Belinda quickly produced. Laurel's hopes for a clean easy escape were thwarted as Cleo caught up with her and hissed. "Don't you dare get temperamental, missy. These guys came all the way from New Orleans to meet you."

"I doubt that, Cleo. If you checked their schedule, you'd probably find they have another assignment in the area. I'm not that important. Now if you'll please excuse me, I'm getting out of here."

"How about later?" She caught Laurel's hand on the door handle. "It really makes me look bad if you don't co-operate."

"I don't care. Just not right now."

"Where can I reach you?"

"At Dane's house." She turned and faced Cleo. "Which also happens to be my house. That bit of information should compensate for my bad attitude. All your nasty little digs have been right. Dane and I have been living to-gether for two and a half months."

"Doesn't surprise me," she gloated. "I thought from the start that you were his live-in. Or live-in-to-be. Now shall we make it four o'clock at the condo?"

"It's not a condo. It's a house, on Cynthia Drive."

"An A-frame house?" Cleo's eyes glittered like that of a cobra about to strike. "Now here's some information for you, sweetheart. That's not Dane's house. It's leased. Probably only for the duration of the Meadow Flowers contract."

"I don't believe that."

"I remember when he was first looking at it. Just before you got here. The rental agent is one of our clients, Law-rence Bell of Bell Homes. I was writing the copy for an ad, and Dane pulled it. Sorry to disappoint you, blondie, but that rustic A-frame, on a heavily wooded cul-de-sac, with two baths, is nothing more than a short-term love nest."

Lawrence Bell? Laurel remembered the name. That was the man Dane had stopped to see when they'd met Doug-las, the little boy who didn't want to get married. Signing a lease, that had been his business with Bell. Even as he had promised to be faithful and honest with her, he had been setting another deception in motion. And this lie was by far the worst.

Laurel jumped into the car. She didn't want to hear any more. What else could there be? He'd lied to her again. It wasn't even his house.

HER SUITCASE was packed. Her plane reservation on the seven o'clock flight to Denver was confirmed. She had changed from her blue silk dress to jeans, a lightweight sweater and a pair of sneakers. All that remained was to say goodbye to Dane.

She wasn't sure whether she was leaving for a week or forever, but she had to go. In Atlanta she'd lost touch with herself. The politely smiling facade had taken over; Laurel needed to shed that image the way a snake wriggles out of its old dead skin. She needed to be alone to find herself again.

In the kitchen she brewed tea—her own mixture of comfrey and rosehips, not Meadow Flowers—in the ceramic pot she'd purchased shortly after moving in with Dane. She knew Cleo was right. This wasn't really Dane's house. That explained why his kitchen had been so sparsely stocked and his closet almost bare when she had first moved in.

The bathroom had been empty, she remembered. Nothing but shaving equipment, toothpaste and deodorant. The medicine cabinet was now full of Dane's cologne and after-shave and bandages. His closet was now so packed with clothing that she had to use the space in the guest bedroom for her rainbow of Meadow Flowers dresses.

There was a new lamp in the front room and magazines stacked neatly under the coffee table. The A-frame house on Cynthia Drive had taken on the lived-in quality of a home. Laurel poured her tea into a thick mug and sweetened it with honey. Why had he deceived her? It was so unnecessary. If he'd told her from the start that he'd just found this house and wanted to share it with her, she would have been deeply touched. Instead she was hurt.

And what about that Thanksgiving car race?

And what about his taste in music? Had the Windham Hill records also been conveniently arranged to suit her preference?

She carried her tea into the front room and sat before the window. The mountain laurel had shed its summer brightness, the delicate branches straining to touch the dusky clouds. Poor tree, she thought, rooted and unable to change except with the season.

Her own season with Dane had been one of great happiness, but perhaps it was time to move on, to find a climate more well suited to her growth. Perhaps there would be snow at the cabin, a thick white blanket to cleanse and purify.

Why hadn't Dane told her about Belinda? And Mort? And his on-going association with the Foster Parents of Atlanta?

Surely such service to others made him proud, and she would have been pleased to share his pride. Even if he'd kept silent out of loyalty to the people he'd helped, he certainly could have spoken about the FPA...unless he didn't trust her.

There was a certain perverted logic to that way of thinking. Though Dane could share his love, he could neither give nor receive trust. His dishonesty robbed them both of dignity and self-respect. He kept himself well hidden behind a three-piece-suit persona that radiated success and power. Why? Laurel hoped the answers would come to her once she'd escaped her own facade.

Dane's BMW was circling the driveway. He parked and walked slowly to the door. His obvious exhaustion tugged at her heartstrings, but she stayed quietly in the chair beside the window.

"Laurel?" he shouted. "I'm home."

"I'm right here."

"Why are you sitting in the dark?"

"I was waiting for sunset, but I guess it's too cloudy."

"A very gray day," he said as he flicked on a lamp.

"I'm leaving, Dane. Going back to Denver on the seven o'clock flight. I was waiting to say goodbye."

He winced as though she'd slapped him. "Is this because of Thanksgiving? If it's that big a deal to you, I'll cancel the whole damn thing."

"My reasons aren't important."

"Of course they are. Tell me why, and I'll make it better. Give me a chance to make things right again."

"Why didn't you tell me? If you'd explained about the Foster Parents Association, I could have forgiven the car race. Why make a secret of your good deeds?"

"Because I'm not some strutting phoney philanthropist. I don't need people to pat me on the back and say 'There goes Dane MacGregor. What a guy!' I hate ceremonial dinners. I don't want to be recognized."

"You'd rather be known as a daredevil pilot? Is that it?"

"Damn right."

She could see the tense working of his jaw. His eyebrows were drawn together, his expression intense. "Let me get this straight. You want to help people, especially people who have been hurt by divorce, but you don't want their gratitude."

"I don't deserve it."

"What?"

"Their problems aren't their fault. They don't have to pay me back."

"But why couldn't you tell me?"

"Maybe I've been carrying this compulsion inside me for too long." He crossed the room and went to the window. His silhouette against the glass made a rigid shadow. "And maybe I didn't want to build myself up too much in your eyes. Didn't want to disappoint you. But I'll try, Laurel. . . . Stay with me, and I'll try to be different."

"My mind is made up. I need to be alone for a while."

"Then you're planning to come back. Just taking a short break?"

"I don't know."

He walked through the house, turning on lights for something to do. In the kitchen beyond her line of vision, he clenched both hands and stopped just short of driving his fist into the solid cedar wall.

He should have known it would come to this, that she'd leave him. Failed. Failed at the one relationship that meant anything to him. Underneath his armor of success, he was still the unlovable little boy who had tidied up his mother's messes.

He poured himself a glass of burgundy and carried it into the front room. "I don't want you to leave."

"I'm sorry."

"I want you to stay with me, to marry me." He drank deeply of the red wine. "Will you marry me? I want to build a life with you, Laurel. I want you to be the mother of our children."

"I can't answer right now. I need time away, alone."

"And what am I supposed to do while you're ruminating at your leisure? Keep the home fires burning until you decide to waltz back into my life?"

"You have to be patient with me."

"To hell with patience!" He flung his glass against the paneled wall. The dregs of wine oozed like blood, staining the wood. "If you walk out on me now, don't bother coming back."

"Maybe I won't."

Laurel was on her feet, visibly shaking. The static in her hair gave her a wild untamed look, and the blue of her eyes pierced through him like butane torches. Oh, God, he thought, she was so beautiful, so good. How could she think of leaving? How could he go on living without her?

"At least tell me why. Why, Laurel?"

"I don't have to tell you anything."

"You owe me that much."

"What is that supposed to mean?" Her voice cracked with emotion. "Are you saying that you took a poor little waif from the wilds of Colorado and made her a star? That you've changed me from a nobody to a success?"

"God, no. That's not what I meant."

"These appearances, these lousy images that are so important to you are nothing to me. You're Mr. Success, but I want the man inside. Not another image."

"You're wrong." He struggled to contain the explosion mounting, rushing within him. His head throbbed with the effort. He felt he was within an inch of madness. His words sounded bitter when he meant them to be a sincere explanation. "I wasn't always Mr. Success, as you call me. I know what it's like to fail. Ten years ago I stood in a bankruptcy court. I sold everything—my furniture, my stereo, my television. My car was repossessed. Maybe you'd like that image better."

"I'm sorry, Dane."

"Or maybe you would have liked me as a dumb little kid. Moving from place to place. Always being in the way. Is that what you would like, Laurel? Some pathetic helpless wimp?"

"Why haven't you told me these things before?"

"Because they're not who I am now."

"But they are. You can't deny your past."

She was right. He knew it. As far as he'd come, as much as he'd changed, he couldn't erase the unlovable child and the destitute man. They were there inside, sabotaging his life. The inadequate pieces of himself were driving her away.

"No!" he shouted. "They aren't me."

The battle within him raged, urging him to strike back. "You're the liar, Laurel. You said you loved me."

"I do. I still love you."

"This isn't how lovers treat each other. People who care about each other don't walk out when things get tough. You can't put limits on your love. It's not fair. Love has to be unconditional."

"There has to be trust on both sides. As long as you keep lying to me, I can't believe in us."

"I've told you everything," he protested. "This Thanksgiving thing isn't that important, is it? Is there something else?"

"I have to go now, Dane. Or I'll miss my plane."

"I meant what I said. If you leave, don't come back."

She picked up her suitcase and walked to the door. "Please, Dane. Don't issue ultimatums that will make it harder for both of us to find a solution."

She left him.

He heard the car door slam and the engine kick into gear. The thrum of the motor faded in the distance, and she was gone.

Slowly Dane knelt on the carpet and picked up the fragments of his shattered wineglass.

12

STRANDED in the Oklahoma City airport, Dane stretched his long legs in front of him and tried to find a comfortable position in the molded plastic chair. It had been sixty-seven hours since Laurel had left him, almost three days. And two long miserable nights.

In a futile attempt to forget her, he had wandered through the house they had shared, drinking glass after glass of wine, turning on the television, then zapping it with the remote control when a Meadow Flowers commercial came on. He'd telephoned Belinda and informed her that all Laurel's appointments were to be postoned for an indefinite period.

"Why is that?"

"She's gone back to Colorado—she wants to find herself—I don't know, maybe she needs to commune with the chipmunks." The wine had gone to his head, making coherent thought difficult. "That's not really why.... There's this guy, this Dane MacGregor, and she can't stand him."

"Are we talking about the same woman?"

"Little blonde? Blue eyes? Stubborn as a mule? Yeah, it's the same one."

"That little blonde was talking about marrying that Dane guy. On the way to the craft fair."

"Oh, God." He had squeezed his eyes shut, fighting to hold back the tears. He hadn't cried in years, couldn't remember the last time he had. *Don't start*, he'd told himself. *Don't start now.* "I guess she changed her mind."

"Do you want some company tonight, Dane? I can be there in about two minutes."

"No. I want to be alone."

"Are you sure? I'm still dressed, and it's no trouble."

"Thanks, lady, but I'll be all right. See you in the morning."

He'd finished the bottle of wine and fallen into a deep dreamless sleep. When he'd wakened two hours later and felt the empty pillow where Laurel's head should have rested, he had wept.

The next day Dane had numbly gone through the motions of running his business. Laurel's name hadn't been mentioned.

Another night. Another day. It had been after five o'clock when the delivery had come from the local florist. No one was left in the office except Belinda. She had tapped on his closed door and entered. "This is for you."

"What the hell is it?"

"Why don't you open it up and find out."

Inside the white cardboard box lay a fragrant white magnolia and a card that read "Be patient, Laurel."

Frantically he'd torn through the flower reference book. What did the white magnolia stand for? He found the notation: perseverance.

As Belinda watched the undignified proceedings, her full lips curved slowly into a smile. "Should I make your plane reservations for Denver?"

"Of course not." He held the creamy white flower to his nose and inhaled the sweet aroma. "What are you talking about?"

"I assume that delivery was from Laurel, because this is the first time since she left that I've seen you excited. Now

I would say that magnolia is a peace offering. The next move is up to you."

"I'll think about it tonight. But if I'm not here in the morning, kill everything on my schedule."

"I'll be happy to." She had pivoted and headed out the door. Over her shoulder she'd tossed a parting comment. "You're a damn fool if you don't go to her."

Dane might be insecure or lacking in self-esteem, but a fool he wasn't. He'd taken the first flight the next morning. Only to be stranded in Oklahoma City while an unseasonably early snowstorm raged in Colorado, forcing the Denver airport to close.

Again he stretched and yawned and rearranged his long frame, mentally cursing the designer who had created airport furniture. It was always uncomfortable and blandly unattractive. And why was it bolted to the floor? Nobody in his right mind would want to steal these hideous plastic contraptions.

He reminded himself that many of the people who came through airports were not sane. Like hijackers. Dane imagined a threatening figure in an army beret leveling a machine gun at him and snarling, "I'll take a hundred thousand in small bills. Or all these chairs will be blown away."

He grinned. That was a good sign. His imagination was beginning to function again. He was sure that seeing Laurel would make everything right.

He planned to be very careful in what he said to her. A fond speech of contrition had begun to form in his mind, which he soon rejected. That wasn't what she wanted.

As amazing as it seemed to him, she wanted him, even after she had learned of his failures. She had told him over and over that she loved the man behind the image, that her only demand was for honesty. Too bad it had taken her absence to convince him.

All his ploys were over, finished and done. He had to tell her everything. The good and the bad. When he'd examined the fabric of his life, trying to patch up the gaping hole left by Laurel's departure, he was surprised at how many good deeds he'd woven into the pattern.

He shook his head. Yet he hadn't told Laurel about those things. She would have been proud of him, but to talk about his generosity, to spread his feathers like a peacock, still seemed pompous and self-righteous. Besides, being an overachiever and a success in business didn't make him a lovable person. He couldn't shake the feeling that he didn't deserve anyone's praise or pride in him. And he had enough lousy acts to his name to undermine any claim to nobility.

Enough of the past. As much as it would hurt, he knew he would have to tell Laurel about the lease on the A-frame house. She'd be mad, but that was better than trying to second guess her. It was important to both of them that he be himself, before it was too late.

That wasn't going to be easy. Dane's whole life had been modeled on a series of images. Even as a little boy he had become the character he had thought his mother would love. Since she'd applauded his performances, the roles had become confused with his identity. He remembered how she had bragged about her son—the straight-A student, the football hero, the president of the senior class.

But there was another memory. After his first business had gone bankrupt and he had visited his mother, she had still loved him. Even though he'd failed. Her darling boy had finally run into a dragon too big to slay, but his mother still believed in him. Her monetary investment had put him back on his feet.

How had he forgotten that? The pain of bankruptcy must have blinded him. He hadn't recognized his mother's unconditional love at the time, just as he hadn't believed in Laurel's love for him. Until now.

He checked his wristwatch. The ticket agent had told him the Denver airport should be open within the hour. An hour had already passed. He toyed with the idea of renting a plane and flying in himself, but rejected it. Laurel would kill him if she ever found out.

He corrected himself—she'd kill him when she found out the far more important things he had to tell her. Because he would tell her, about the house and his insecurities. There could be no more secrets between them. No more lies.

LAUREL THREW another log on the blazing fire and returned to the kitchen, where a large pot of creamy potato soup simmered. She regretted that she hadn't spent the first day after her arrival winterizing the cabin. She really should have hooked up the generator that Dane had arranged to be delivered to her cabin and tacked heavy-duty plastic over the windows for an extra layer of insulation. Who would have expected such a heavy snow in mid-November?

Above the timberline this wouldn't be unusual weather. In Laurel's valley, however, the snow seldom accumulated before December. She gazed through the kitchen windows. What a beautiful sight! The fury of the storm had abated to a gentle sifting of large white flakes. Luckily she'd stocked up on provisions the day before, when she had also ordered the magnolia blossom for Dane.

What would he do, she wondered, when he received her note? She halfway hoped he'd disregard her message to wait patiently and dash to her side. But the snow had eliminated that possibility. The stretch of road up to her cabin was closed with high drifts.

Wanting quiet and solitude, Laurel hadn't told her family she was back in Colorado. Maybe next week she would surprise them with a visit. But what could she say? Two days' rest wasn't enough to disentangle herself from her Atlanta image, and she was a long way from making any decisions about her life.

The only person she'd talked to had been Annie Terrance, an awkward conversation over the telephone at the grocery store. And that had been a gloomy conversation. Annie had just broken up with her lawyer boyfriend because—of all reasons—they were too much alike. According to Annie, the relationship had ended because there was no spontaneity or spark.

Laurel mused on the contrast between her and Annie as she stirred the potato soup with a long wooden spoon. Spark was certainly not missing in her relationship with Dane. At times their differences led to full-scale conflagrations.

She loved him, but she wasn't sure if she could live with him. He'd talked about love without conditions, and she agreed in theory with that philosophy. It was unfair to demand changes in another person, to say, "I'll love you only if . . ."

Reality was another matter. It wasn't easy to love Dane when he kept himself so well camouflaged. Love was not a path to be taken lightly, not with all the obstacles he created. Yet it was the route she truly desired to follow. Somewhere she would find the tolerance and understanding to help him put an end to lies.

And the first deception to erase was their living together arrangement. Laurel knew that they had to be married, seriously dedicated to their relationship. For better or worse. It had to be marriage or a clean break.

If he ever agreed to see her again, that was. Wedding plans were somewhat premature when the last words he'd spoken to her were "Don't come back."

The thought of their final argument chilled Laurel more than the freezing temperatures outside. A life without Dane? Impossible! They had to reconcile. There had to be a way.

She left the kitchen and eased herself into a rocking chair in front of the fireplace. Her thighs ached pleasantly from the hiking she'd done the morning after her arrival at the cabin. The day had been sunny, and she had been drawn to the field where she had first heard the whir of Dane's ultralight. . . .

Sitting with her boots propped up before the fire, she sighed. Hard to believe it had only been three months since they'd met. It seemed like several lifetimes ago. So much had happened that she felt compelled to catalogue the events—the make over, Meadow Flowers, the A-frame house, Atlanta, dinners and luncheons and autographs and television commercials and crowds.

That life was the extreme opposite of the Rocky Mountain solitude she enjoyed at the cabin. Here the biggest event of the month would be the early snowfall, casting its silent blanket over the valley.

Laurel rose and began to pace restlessly. If she had to choose between the two lives, she didn't know which she would pick. The high excitement, the attention accorded the Meadow Flowers spokeswoman, had invigorated her. Yet she also needed the inner peace that came from absolute quiet.

But what about Dane? She needed him, too.

She checked her supply of wood. Since the fire had to be kept burning all night, she would need a couple of big logs from the shed. It was late afternoon already. Time to light up the kerosene lamps and fetch wood.

She pulled on her heavy parka and stepped outside. Through knee-deep snow she trudged to the shed, pushed the door and gathered up two thick logs. Twice more she made the trek, depositing her wood on the porch. On her fourth and final journey, she paused. There was a whining sound against the wind. Were the snow plows coming to clear the roads? She didn't think so. The plows made a heavier rumbling noise.

She stared through the stand of pine trees. It wasn't a car or a jeep. And it certainly couldn't be any sort of aircraft in this weather.

Abruptly Laurel dropped her logs, then waded through three-foot-high drifts toward the impassable road leading to her cabin. Joyful anticipation surged through her as the icy wind whipped against her cheeks.

In a burst of color the snowmobile flew over the last hill toward her house. The driver wore an orange suit, matching moon boots and goggles. He was covered from head to toe, but Laurel knew him immediately.

"Dane!" she cried, trying to run toward him and falling face-down in the deep snow.

He parked, killed the engine and was beside her in an instant. They embraced on their knees in the snow, oblivious to the freezing temperatures, too ecstatically happy to move.

Tears of happiness mingled with the snowflakes on Laurel's cheeks. Through numbed lips she whispered, "I was afraid you wouldn't come."

"You don't disapprove of snowmobiles?"

"Of course I disapprove. They rut the fields and frighten the animals. But I wouldn't care if you had driven here on an MX missile as long as you got here in one piece."

"What are you doing outside in the snow?"

"Waiting for you."

"It is all right if we go inside, isn't it?"

They made a wide path to the door, stomping and giggling like children. He carried the logs in, in one trip, and dumped them beside the fire.

His gear had protected him more thoroughly than her jeans, parka and boots. As he slid the goggles off and unzipped his orange nylon snow suit, he said with concern, "You're wet."

"Only on my legs."

"Go change. I don't want you to catch a cold."

"What if I just take off everything?" she suggested with a smirk, trying to coax him out of his sudden reserve. "You could join me under the goose-down quilt."

"That's a hell of a good idea," he said with a warmth that set her blood simmering. "But first we need to talk."

She changed rapidly, a million possibilities crashing through her brain. She warned herself to be sensible. Then contradicted that advice with a surge of pure love for him. Only Dane would be capable of such a dramatic entrance.

Of course they needed to talk, she told herself. They needed to map out their future, but somehow all the questions and answers seemed redundant. Once she had seen him she realized their love was the treasure that all fortune seekers hoped for—a precious priceless jewel with every facet reflecting so beautifully that the flaws were inconsequential.

When Laurel came back downstairs she found Dane in the kitchen, starting the kettle for tea.

"The first thing," he said, catching sight of her, "is that I've been sneaking cups of coffee on the sly. And I intend to keep on drinking coffee despite your disapproval of caffeine."

"I can live with that. In fact, some people think caffeine is a sexual stimulant."

"The second thing is about the stock-car race on Thanksgiving Day. I've planned it. I've done it for four years in a row, and it's of great benefit to the FPA. The race goes on, Laurel. It's not fair to those foster parents and kids to call it off. They depend on that money for their programs."

"I agree."

"You do? Why couldn't you have said that in Atlanta? Not that I haven't been thrilled to pieces by this cross-country trek in the snow."

"It wasn't the race itself that I objected to."

She tried to be serious, to wipe the silly smile from her face. These were important concerns they were discussing, but she was so glad to see him that grins and giggles bubbled through her cool demeanor.

"What was it that you objected to then?"

"The fact that you didn't tell me. You didn't trust me enough to think I'd be understanding about a charity event. Mind you, Dane, I really wish you wouldn't join in the race. I still hate the idea of daredevil risks."

"That's simple enough," he said. "I'll consider withdrawing from the race. On one condition: you come with me and take a look at all the safety devices and protective mechanisms. Remember, Laurel, we're not talking about the Indy 500 here. These are stock, standard-issue automobiles. If you're still not convinced about safety, I'll withdraw from the race."

"Fine." She took the whistling kettle off the stove and made the tea.

"There's something else," he said. "Something very important...."

She held her breath. Was he going to tell her about the house? Without prompting, would he reveal this, the final deception that had truly sabotaged their relationship?

"It's about the house on Cynthia Drive.... It's not my house. It belongs to a contractor who does his advertising through us. Do you remember Douglas, the little boy who wanted to wash my car? Well, while you were talking to him, I was leasing the house from Lawrence Bell. Remember how tired I was the next morning? I told you that my exhaustion was from sexual frustration—partly true, as a matter of fact—but I had also spent the night moving furniture."

"I know about the house."

"What?"

"Cleo told me right after the craft fair."

"And that was really why you left, wasn't it? Because I'd lied to you about something as basic as where I lived."

"Why did you do it, Dane?" She handed him his mug of tea and nodded toward the other room. "Let's sit by the fire. I have a feeling this might be a long explanation."

Once they had settled into rocking chairs he began. "I wanted to impress you, and my condo isn't your style. I wanted you to think I was the sort of man who lived in a rustic A-frame. I even went out and bought those mellow Windham Hill records. Do you think, Laurel, that you'll ever be able to trust me again?"

"It depends," she teased. "What kind of music do you really like?"

"Folk singers. Like Gordon Lightfoot and Judy Collins."

" 'Send in the Clowns,' " she said.

"There's a lot in that song that applies to us."

"Indeed, there is. We're really quite a pair."

"Can there be smiles for us, Laurel? Or should I ride off into the sunset on my snowmobile?"

"I want you to trust me. That's the real problem, Dane. It's not that I don't trust you, but the other way around. All these deceptions happen because you don't really believe in me. Or in my love for you. It doesn't matter to me where you live or what you wear or if you drink coffee. When I say that I love you, I'm not putting conditions on it."

"I think I understand that now, but it's still hard to accept. My life has been spent proving myself, manufacturing images for people to admire and care about."

"And hiding yourself," she completed his thought.

"I want to change, Laurel. The only place I want to lie is in your bed."

"Not quite yet," she said tenderly. "Finish your tea. I need to absorb all this."

She gazed into the fire, mesmerized by its crackling everchanging form. A miracle, really. Fire.

Almost as miraculous as this talk. Everything had turned out beautifully. As long as they could both remember the love they shared, their differences would be consumed, as the logs would be turned into wispy smoke by the flames. Though she was certain they would disagree at times, the future seemed as bright and cozy as the hearthside.

"I have a few more questions," she said. "But I don't have the answers. For instance, I liked the work I did with Meadow Flowers, but I also like living in the mountains."

"I know geography is not your forte," Dane teased her. "But Atlanta is not at all far from the Blue Ridge mountains. It might just be possible for us to find ourselves a little plot of land and build a cabin."

"By ourselves."

"I don't pretend to know anything about carpentry and sinking wells," he admitted. "But they say ignorance is bliss."

"And when would we be able to visit this unbuilt edifice? If I remember correctly, you have quite a busy schedule."

"Whenever we wanted to. I just spent two days in the office, but not in the office, if you know what I mean. When I wasn't staring into space I was yelling about some inconsequential matter. And do you know what happened? Nothing. Business went on as usual. People still did their jobs. Sales were closed and deals consummated. I'm going to name Belinda the new vice-president and office manager. She's doing the work, anyway."

"She told me about what you did for her."

He slapped his hand against his thigh. "I knew there was something else I hadn't told you about. Do you want to hear about Mort? Or Carlos the stock boy? Or about—"

"Whoa! How many times have you stepped in and changed somebody's life?"

"Seven or eight. But I don't want you to think of this as admirable. My insecurity has always spurred me on. I've always needed to be a hero, and all these people were ripe for a rescue mission."

He grinned at her. Even if he hadn't spent the better part of the day climbing to Rocky Mountain altitude, he would have been on top of the world. Though he had expected arguments, she'd given understanding. And love. Never again would he look into those sky-blue eyes and not see trust shining from them.

"Rescue mission?" she questioned sardonically.

"Captain Dane," he proclaimed himself. "Do you think you could whip me up a Superhero outfit? Yellow tights and a cape?"

"Another identity? You have more disguises than a porcupine has quills. Now get serious."

"I don't want to be serious." He finished his tea in a gulp and leaped to his feet, gesturing dramatically. "I want to right every wrong. To fight every battle, to slay every dragon. For truth, justice and the American way."

"All right, Captain Dane," she said, playing along. "What motivated you to help all those people?"

"Captain Dane has the magic formula—known to earthlings as ready cash. Because of his disjointed childhood, when many fathers joined with his supermom, Captain Dane is sensitive to the hurt caused by broken homes. Tell me, madam, if you were confronted with a situation that could be solved by giving someone a job or finding them a home or buying them a plane ticket, wouldn't you help?"

She set down her tea and walked toward him. Wrapping her arms around his neck, she fluttered her eyelashes and said, "My hero."

"I certainly hope so." He dropped the pose and hugged her tightly. "I can't believe it, Laurel. This couldn't have worked out better if I'd planned it. Which I didn't, by the way. I came to you with high hopes and a resolve to trust. No more schemes. You will notice how straightforwardly I am carrying you up to the bedroom," he went on. "No subtlety and no deception. Lady, I want you."

"Good! I've always wondered what Superheroes were like under their tights."

Upstairs it was chilly, and they wasted no time divesting themselves of clothing and diving under the goose-down quilt. There were two layers of wool blankets under the warm mauve quilt, and the sheets were soft flannel.

She snuggled up to him. "For body heat," she assured him.

"This is cozy. . . ."

"Hmm. . . . Now that you're here, it's wonderful."

"Shall we build a fire? Let's see how well I remember my Boy Scout training."

"You were a Boy Scout?"

"Hey, you're talking to one real-live overachiever. I was an Eagle Scout." He made tiny quick strokes on her breast, teasing the nipple to hardness as he explained, "This is the kindling."

He kissed her, a gentle possession of her lips that deepened as his tongue slid past the smooth white barrier of her teeth and found its willing mate. When they parted he breathed into her ear, "Those were the heavier twigs and branches."

"I can't wait for the big logs," she said.

"But you can, and you will."

In their months of living together he had learned the secrets of her pleasure. With an intensity heightened by deliberate slowness, he fondled her breasts and stroked the insides of her thighs.

Laurel responded with her own skillful touch, finding the spot at the base of his spine that caused him to stiffen and shudder against her.

When finally he entered her, the heat generated by their bodies was so fierce that he tossed aside the covers, joining with her in strong hard thrusts. Together they rose to climax, a physical flowering of their love.

Afterward they nestled in each other's arms, once again under the warm nest of blankets. Laurel ran her hand fondly over his cheek and said softly, "I forgot to mention one tiny thing in our fireside chat."

"What's that, darling? Would you like the moon to wear, on a silver chain around your neck? Name it, and it's yours."

"I want to marry you."

The quiet in her pine-paneled bedroom was almost complete. Only distant crackling from the fireplace downstairs accompanied the gentle beating of their hearts. Outside, dusk was falling, leaving barely enough light from the windows to discern his features. Yet she thought his smile was the most wonderful sight she'd ever seen.

"Wait right here," he said.

"Dane?" she called after his quickly retreating figure as he hurried down the stairs. "Where are you going?"

She flopped back against the pillows and yawned contentedly. The man was definitely a lunatic, but he was her lunatic. She reached out from the covers and lighted the kerosene lamp at her bedside. From downstairs she heard the sound of zippers being opened and closed. What could he be doing?

She heard him thundering up the stairs and looked up to see him hovering over the bed, beautifully naked. His hands were behind his back.

"Do you know how many pockets those snowmobile suits have? Must be at least eight big ones."

"Get under the covers before you freeze."

"Not yet."

The flowers and leaves he scattered over the quilt were somewhat mashed from their journey but still beautiful and fragrant.

"Orange blossoms . . ." she murmured.

He dove under the covers and found her left hand. Onto the fourth finger he slipped a golden ring. The design was a laurel wreath, the age-old symbol of honor and glory.

Harlequin Temptation

COMING NEXT MONTH

#105 THE SKY'S THE LIMIT
Jill Bloom

Charlotte could navigate a plane around the world, yet she couldn't chart a steady course with Bobby. She needed a friend, a kindred spirit, a mechanic.... Did she need a lover, too?

#106 AFTER THE RAIN
Madeline Harper

Emma Dixon's foray into the jungles of the Yucatán was not without incident. Adventure and intrigue followed fast on her heels—as did the attractive and virile Jack Winston.

#107 HOOK, LINE AND SINKER
Lynn Turner

Turning city slicker Travis McCauley into a fisherman and all-round nature boy was a challenge Mica couldn't resist. He'd brought his own very special lures....

#108 CAPTIVATED
Carla Neggers

He had style; she had nerve. Together Richard and Sheridan were winners in a real-life cops and robbers game. Their biggest gamble was with each other....

Take 4 books
& a surprise gift
FREE

1. How do you rate _____
   (Please print book TITLE)

   1.6 ☐ excellent   .4 ☐ good   .2 ☐ not so good
   .5 ☐ very good   .3 ☐ fair   .1 ☐ poor

2. How likely are you to purchase another book:
   in this *series* ?   by this *author* ?
   2.1 ☐ definitely would purchase   3.1 ☐ definitely would purchase
   .2 ☐ probably would puchase   .2 ☐ probably would puchase
   .3 ☐ probably would not purchase   .3 ☐ probably would not purchase
   .4 ☐ definitely would not purchase   .4 ☐ definitely would not purchase

   B12345678

3. How does this book compare with similar books you usually read?
   4.1 ☐ far better than others   .2 ☐ better than others   .3 ☐ about the
   .4 ☐ not as good   .5 ☐ definitely not as good   same

4. Please check the statements you feel best describe this book.
   5. ☐ Easy to read   6. ☐ Too much violence/anger
   7. ☐ Realistic conflict   8. ☐ Wholesome/not too sexy
   9. ☐ Too sexy   10. ☐ Interesting characters
   11. ☐ Original plot   12. ☐ Especially romantic
   13. ☐ Not enough humor   14. ☐ Difficult to read
   15. ☐ Didn't like the subject   16. ☐ Good humor in story
   17. ☐ Too predictable   18. ☐ Not enough description of setting
   19. ☐ Believable characters   20. ☐ Fast paced
   21. ☐ Couldn't put the book down 22. ☐ Heroine too juvenile/weak/silly
   23. ☐ Made me feel good   24. ☐ Too many foreign/unfamiliar words
   25. ☐ Hero too dominating   26. ☐ Too wholesome/not sexy enough
   27. ☐ Not enough romance   28. ☐ Liked the setting
   29. ☐ Ideal hero   30. ☐ Heroine too independent
   31. ☐ Slow moving   32. ☐ Unrealistic conflict
   33. ☐ Not enough suspense   34. ☐ Sensuous/not too sexy
   35. ☐ Liked the subject   36. ☐ Too much description of setting

5. What *most* prompted you to buy this book?
   37. ☐ Read others in series   38. ☐ Title   39. ☐ Cover art
   40. ☐ Friend's recommendation 41. ☐ Author   42. ☐ In-store display
   43. ☐ TV, radio or magazine ad 44. ☐ Price   45. ☐ Story outline
   46. ☐ Ad inside other books   47. ☐ Other _____ (please specify)

6. Please indicate how many romance paperbacks you read in a month .
   48.1 ☐ 1 to 4   .2 ☐ 5 to 10   .3 ☐ 11 to 15   .4 ☐ more than 15

7. Please indicate your sex and age group.
   49.1 ☐ Male   50.1 ☐ under 15   .3 ☐ 25-34   .5 ☐ 50-64
   .2 ☐ Female   .2 ☐ 15-24   .4 ☐ 35-49   .6 ☐ 65 or older

8. Have you any additional comments about this book?
   _____ (51)
   _____ (53)

Thank you for completing and returning this questionnaire.
Printed in USA

NAME _____
(Please Print)

ADDRESS _____

CITY _____

ZIP CODE _____

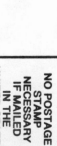

BUSINESS REPLY MAIL

FIRST CLASS   PERMIT NO. 70   TEMPE, AZ.

POSTAGE WILL BE PAID BY ADDRESSEE

NATIONAL READER SURVEYS

2504 West Southern Avenue
Tempe, AZ   85282

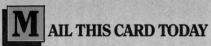

M AIL THIS CARD TODAY

You'll receive 4 Harlequin novels
plus a fabulous surprise gift
ABSOLUTELY FREE

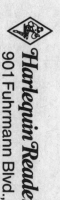

Harlequin Reader Service
901 Fuhrmann Blvd.,
P.O. Box 1394
Buffalo, NY 14240-9963

BUSINESS REPLY CARD

First Class   Permit No. 717   Buffalo, NY

Postage will be paid by addressee

4 EXCITING ROMANCE NOVELS PLUS A SURPRISE GIFT

FREE BOOKS/ SURPRISE GIFT

YES, please send me my four **FREE** Harlequin Temptations™ and my **FREE** surprise gift. Then send me four brand-new Harlequin Temptations each month as soon as they come off the presses. Bill me at the low price of $1.99 each (for a total of $7.95 — a saving of $1.04 off the retail price). There are no shipping, handling or other hidden costs. There is no minimum number of books I must purchase. I can always return a shipment and cancel at any time. Even if I never buy a book from Harlequin, the four free novels and the surprise gift are mine to keep forever.

142 CIX MDKW

NAME_____

ADDRESS_____APT. NO._____

CITY_____

STATE_____ZIP_____

Offer limited to one per household and not valid for present subscribers. Prices subject to change.

Mail to:
Harlequin Reader Service
901 Fuhrmann Blvd.
P.O. Box 1394
Buffalo, NY 14240
U.S.A.

LIMITED TIME ONLY
Mail today and get a
SECOND MYSTERY GIFT

Irresistible!